LOVE'S FIRST CHAPTER

by

Antoinette Muse

DORRANCE
PUBLISHING CO
EST. 1920
PITTSBURGH, PENNSYLVANIA 15238

Dorrance Publishing Co
585 Alpha Drive
Pittsburgh, PA 15238
Visit our website at www.dorrancebookstore.com

ISBN: 979-8-88925-269-6
eISBN: 979-8-88925-769-1

Chapter 1

Philippians 2:3–4 (ESV)

3 Do nothing from selfish ambition or conceit, but in humility count others more significant than yourselves. 4 Let each of you look not only to his own interests, but also to the interests of others.

The alarm clock's incessant buzzing lasted for approximately five minutes before Joelle realized she wasn't dreaming. She rolled over in her king-sized bed that was littered with a dozen or so pink and green pillows for decoration purposes only to glance at the time. It was now 6:30 a.m. The eighty-two-inch window-darkening apple green curtains on her bedroom windows did a great job of blocking out the morning rays that would have been a beacon letting her know it was time to get up. Joelle rolled back over and opened one eye. Her spacious bedroom looked massive when looking out one eye. She had just enough pieces in the room to fill out the space nicely. She opted for oak-wood white furniture to match the pink and green decor. Her favorite piece was a light pink leather lounge chaise at the base of the bed. Her mother thought she was crazy for purchasing it, but Joelle didn't care.

Her light gray walls were adorned with the artwork of local Black artists. Joelle found three pieces by three artists that really complimented each other. The first were of praying hands. Joelle, a devout Christian, loved having pieces that worshipped God. That is why she choose the second piece that featured open hands signifying come. She could tell the hands were supposed to be those of Jesus offering salvation to men, women, and children. Her third piece was simply a bible. Over this one, Joelle installed a light to shine directly on it. It reminded Joelle to seek the Lord when she was having a problem or concern.

She paid the most for this particular piece and felt it was worth every penny. Many a day, she came home and fell into her chaise lounge crying over something, person, or situation. She gazed at the portrait and then grabbed her bible from the drawer attached to the bottom of the chaise and started reading God's word.

She didn't always understand the passage God directed her to at the moment, but during the week, God would reveal His will and the way Joelle needed to proceed with handling the person or situation. In addition to this, she often cozied up on the chaise when watching Netflix or Hulu on her fifty-five-inch TV.

Joelle knew that she should get up, but instead she hit the Snooze button one last time. In exactly eight minutes, she would get her day started. When Joelle looked over at the clock again it read 7:00 a.m.

"Damn it!" This time she slept through the alarm's buzzing; unfortunately thirty minutes elapsed before her internal clock finally woke her. Joelle jumped up and barely missed colliding with Jinx, her overfed, over-finicky monster of a cat. Joelle ran over to open the curtains to let God's light into her bedroom. Her apartment overlooked the park on Ben Franklin Parkway. She paid a pretty penny for this apartment, but she loved the views from all of her windows. She told herself she would run on Philadelphia's famous Boat House Row every day. In three years, she had failed to step on foot on concrete for a run, walk, heck not even a skip. But she knew there was always time.

"Move it, Jinx!" Joelle said.

Jinx scurried his all-black frame across the floor and took his place at his breakfast bowl in the kitchen. Joelle knew that if she did not stop to feed him at that exact moment, he would meow her to death. Joelle followed him into her kitchen, which was the smallest room in the apartment. Joelle, not being much of a cook, was completely happy with its size. She had cherry red cabinets. All of her appliances were chrome and they were in a perfect square with the island in the center of the room that housed a double sink and a sliver of counter space for a dish dryer and utensil container full of gadgets she has never used. Joelle couldn't peel a potato, but she had a potato peeler. Again, something she would have to add to her list of things to do. She quickly pulled Jinx's expensive food from the top shelf of her cabinet. She heaped out three healthy portions of the dried cat food into Jinx's favorite 14 karat gold-plated bowl. She knew the feeding bowl was a bit excessive, however, she did not care. Jinx was her baby and he deserved the best.

She reminisced back to when she found Jinx. She literally found him in a cardboard box three blocks from her house on her way home from work. There was a handwritten sign that said *Free Cats* taped to both sides of the box. Jinx must have been the one that no one else wanted because he was the only one left. He was all black with emerald green eyes. Joelle's grandfather had once told her that he would put his car into reverse if a black cat crossed his path while driving. Joelle did not share his perspective on black cats. After all, the cat didn't create itself. Joelle grabbed the cuddly, affectionate kitten from out of the box and never looked back. She snuck him into her apartment through the back entrance. There was no way she was going to pay the two-hundred dollar pet fee asked by her apartment complex. She had the money, but she felt since she didn't have to pay for a human companion, why pay for a furry one. No one would even know the cat was there. She purchased all the necessary items and decided on Jinx as the name. Despite the irony, she felt lucky to have found him when she did.

"You better not eat this too fast. I don't plan on cleaning up vomit this evening when I get home. Fat cat!"

Jinx looked up and rolled his eyes as if Joelle's words were more of a nuisance than a threat. After feeding Jinx, Joelle ran into the bathroom. She cut the water on full blast and quickly removed her matching bra and panty set. Any other time, she would have loved the massage provided by the six shower heads dispensing water from all angles, but not today. Joelle kicked her underwear aside and stepped into the shower, glad she wasn't confined by pajamas the night before so as to expedite the bathing process. She never liked wearing pajamas to bed anyway; she felt restricted. When she was a girl, her mother would constantly nag her about wearing pajamas or a night shirt at the very least. Joelle was the youngest and in a household of male siblings. Her oldest brother, Joshua Jr, seven years her senior, was out of the house and in the military by the time Joelle's body started maturing and requiring a cover-up. That left her with Jacob and Jonah. Jacob would be celebrating his thirty-fourth birthday in June, while Jonah just turned thirty-one last month. Joelle, at twenty-nine, was always reminded that a proper lady never slept in underwear apparel only by her mother and other maternal-like figures in her life. It just wasn't done.

Joelle glanced at the built-in clock on the tiled wall of the shower and quickly jumped out.

"Seven thirty.... Oh crap. Where did the time go?"

Jinx licked the remnants of his breakfast from his mouth and retired to his spot on Joelle's massive king-size mahogany bed.

Joelle pulled her two-piece pin-striped black and white pants suit from her walk-in closet. She quickly found a pair of matching pumps, grabbed her briefcase, and hurried out the door. Her Uber should be there any minute according to her app. She was hoping her father was making rounds instead of being stationed at the receptionist area today so she could slip in unnoticed. She can't be late today. She locked the door and rushed down the steps and exited the building, but not without saying good morning to Jonathan the doorman.

Her heels step off the rug in front of the building and onto the concrete. As she walks around the corner towards the parking garage, she hears a faint noise from a box on the side of the garage entrance. It's similar to the box she found Jinx in. In her head she knew she didn't have time to investigate any further. She glanced at her watch. If she left right now, she would only be ten minutes late. But then it meowed and melted her heart. There was no time to take it to a shelter. She couldn't possibly take it to work with her. After all, she needs to uphold her reputation of taking her job seriously. But she couldn't leave it outside all alone. She remembered being alone before Jinx who offered her unconditional love.

Joelle had had many opportunities for love to blossom in the past. However, most of her suitors were more interested in her family fortune than her. After the first few went horribly left, she would put off telling them any particulars about her family until the fourth date. Unfortunately, once they found out that she was the only daughter to Joshua Jamison, Sr., Joelle took a back seat and greed took her place, thus ruining the relationship. Joelle tried to play down her family fortune but to no avail; especially since her parents were often featured in the local financial magazine as well as global publications. She thought she saw something special in her last boyfriend, Bryan. Joelle thought he was different and in it for the long haul. After he successfully made it through to the fourth date without showing any inkling of being interested in her family's status, Joelle thought he was a keeper and definitely husband material. She decided to invite him to the annual Christmas party to see how he handled himself in front of her family.

She already had explained her job to him, but she played it down a lot. He had no idea that she was in charge of her division. Even though he had a good job as a firefighter for the city of Philadelphia, she knew most men were intimidated by successful women that made a six-figure salary. It didn't hit him just how successful she was until he stepped into the foyer of Jamison Communications where he saw a picture of the family on one accent wall in the foyer. He completely freaked out. He apologized and told her he could not see her again. And like that, he was gone. The next day, Joelle stumbled upon the box of free kittens. She and Jinx had been inseparable since that fateful day. She knew that Jinx was no accident and that he would be there through the test of time. She put the furry creature in her purse and headed to Walgreens to get some food and water. She jumped back into the car and started the engine.

"Oh boy, that took way longer than I thought."

Joelle put on her turn signal and maneuvered into traffic and headed towards her office, praying that God would provide a miracle.

Chapter 2

Xavier unlocked the front door to When the Saints Go Marchin' In bookstore and quickly disarmed the alarm. The last time he failed to deactivate it in the allotted time, Philadelphia's finest were sent out to his establishment with guns drawn. After providing his ID and showing them his keys, he was able to convince them that he was, in fact, the owner of the store. Even though he was agitated, he gave them a ten percent coupon to purchase anything once the store opened in two months. He was trying to change the perception that Black men could not be business owners, so he figured he would start with the police.

Although he was happy his establishment was high on the authorities' priority chain, he also knew that the location was the main reason behind their immediate attention. He purchased space in the trendy art museum section of the city. At first, he was apprehensive given that he was unsure if a Christian bookstore would do well in the area. He thought about having secular books, but he didn't feel God called him to include them in his store. He was paying little to nothing in rent since the owner just needed someone in the spot to prevent the property from getting broken into when the police were not canvasing his area. The lease was year to year, which worked for both parties. Xavier wouldn't want to close if his business venture proved unfruitful, but if he had to, he would be able to do so without any penalties related to breaking the lease. He was hopeful that he would be able to minister to the community and make a profit at the same time. He wasn't looking to become rich; he just wanted to make a good return on his investment and praise God by bringing the word to the community.

He tossed the keys and his morning paper on the unfinished counter. He was in awe as he looked at the progress the contractors had made on his baby. All the sweat and pain Xavier put into his bookstore really made it feel as if he had given birth to a new life. Of course, it wasn't flesh and blood, but it was a new creation.

"Xavier, I see you staring up at the old rugged cross again. Have you received your calling?"

Xavier looked into his father's eyes and couldn't help but chuckle. James Lawerence was all of six foot four and approximately 260 lbs. However, standing over Xavier, all X could think about was when he was six years old and his father wore a clown outfit to his birthday party. The costume came equipped with high waters, suspenders, and a polka dot necktie. He looked like a version of the character from Tyler Perry's *Meet the Browns*, ashy knees and all. Everyone at the party laughed at James, including Xavier's brother, Xavian, and his sister, Xeria. James always knew how to make his children laugh and being a single parent, he knew the importance of providing a nurturing environment for his children.

Xavier's mom, Jamiah, died when Xeria was born. Xavier was sandwiched between Xavian two years his senior and Xeria four years younger. Xavier, who was affectionately called X by his loved ones, remembered the day James brought Xeria home wrapped in a pink blanket. Ms. Martha was watching the two brothers while they patiently waited for their parents to come home from the hospital. At four years old, X was excited to meet his little sister, but he was curious as to why his mother hadn't brought Xeria into the house instead of James. At first X, thought his mom was out getting something out of the car for his adorable little sister. He learned differently later after she hadn't come into the home within ten to fifteen minutes. James was busy getting his little sister settled into the pink and white nursery he and his mother had set up for her a week prior to her coming home.

James sat X and his brother Xavian down and explained that their mother had gone on to glory to be with Jesus. X didn't quite understand what that meant, but when he saw tears falling from Xavian's eyes, he knew his life would forever be changed. James didn't go into any details, but only said there were complications. When the three were all in their twenties, X asked his father for more details concerning his mother's premature passing. Even though he didn't want to have his father relive those tragic memories, he needed to know what happened to his beloved mother. James told them he knew one day he would have to share what really happened with his children. James explained that Jamiah developed an infection soon after she gave birth to Xeria.

James was told by her doctors that this was a common occurrence and he was reassured that she would be okay. He kissed his wife and was asked to wait outside. He went to check on Xeria in the hospital nursery and then he sat in the waiting room. When the chief attending for the OB GYN department approached him he could tell something was wrong. The doctor explained that the infection had spread to other parts of her body rapidly. They tried their best, but they were unable to stop the infection from spreading to her vital organs. X could tell from the tears swelling up in his father's eyes, that he was still devastated by her loss.

James stated that he sobbed for an hour in the waiting room. He begged God that the doctors were wrong or at best talking about someone else's wife. Not his beloved queen, life partner, his Eve. As he sat there in the most sterile waiting room he had ever been in, James heard a voice from God telling him *Be Still and Know that I am God.*

He wiped his eyes and again went to visit his angel Xeria in the nursery. Even though he still had fears of raising three children alone, he knew that the fears would not consume him. With God's help, the four of them would be okay. With every birthday party, James went all out to show his children they were loved enough for both a mother and a father. Xavian and Xavier stepped up to the plate also when it came to Xeria. They were super protective of her back then and still to this very day. The three siblings are extremely close. Xavian, now thirty-four, along with his wife Julia, thirty-two, host a family dinner every Sunday at their house in the Bala Cynwood area of the city. Like his father, Xavian who accepted his calling, is now the pastor of New Life Baptist on Fifty-Fourth Street. James thought that Xavian would take over as pastor of his church, Living Vine, but instead he took over as pastor of New Life when approached by a deacon from that church. James was disappointed. With Xavian at New Life, James was hopeful that Xavier would follow both men's footstep if God called him and take over as the pastor of Living Vine when James retired. But he never pressured Xavier.

Xavian and Julia had twin six-year old-boys, Justin and Julian. X loved spending time with his nephews, but at thirty-two, he was not necessarily ready to settle down like his brother. He did however take comfort in the idea of having a brood of little Xs running around one day. The weekly family dinners were a way for the family to stay connected given all had busy schedules. X loved them, and when the time came for him to settle down, he would love to have his wife and children sit at the table with his siblings' families and the patriarch, James. Xeria would always show up half an hour late to the gatherings with some elaborate excuse for her tardiness. This would have the entire group including her overprotective father with eyebrows raised.

Chapter 3

Joelle pulled into the parking lot of Jamison Telecommunications at 9:15 a.m. She grabbed her briefcase with one hand and secured the tote bag she found on her back seat with the kitten and food inside on her left shoulder. Joelle decided that there was no sense in running since she was already late. And she didn't want to unnerve the kitten to the point where it began to vocalize its anxiety.

A sense of relief came across her face when she saw that her father was not standing at the door or the receptionist desk. Joelle at five seven, was light on her feet. She glided through the office with ease as if she was on time. She made sure to say hello to her fellow coworkers. She reached her office and her administrative assistant met her at the door with a slight frown on her face.

"Good Morning, Stella! How are you doing this fine day?"

"Joelle, you know you are pushing it. Your 9:00 a.m. appointment is waiting for you in the conference room and your father wants you to call him as soon as the meeting is over. The other messages will have to wait until after your meeting. Now get going." She gave Joelle's the folder with the clients' name, pointed her in the right direction, and gave her a light shove. Stella was almost twice her age. She had started with the company while Joelle was away at college. She knew her father assigned Stella to her because she was the mother figure that Joelle needed to keep her organized and on top of her game. Joelle was thankful that she worked with her and not for her.

" Wait Stella, I need your help with something."

Joelle handed her the tote bag. Stella looked in the bag and nodded her head. She turned and walked away towards her office. Stella required no more instructions. Joelle didn't have to micromanage her and trusted she would have this situation taken care while Joelle was in her meeting. As she scurried off, she dreaded the conversation she would be having with her father later. For now, she needed to put her game face on and go to work to make that paper, cheddar, greenbacks, duckets, and any other slang the kids were using to refer to money.

"Yes! I snagged the Mott Hotel."

Joelle wanted to jump up and down, but she didn't want to make a spectacle of herself. What the hell, she looked around and then decided to go for it. She let out a tiny squeal of excitement. She then looked at the contract between Jamison Telecommunications and The Mott Hotel, which included several multi-line phone systems in three conference rooms and the front reception lobby; and two phones in each of their 200 guest bed rooms. Joelle had been working on this project for months. This acquisition just hauled in two million dollars to Jamison Telecommunications. This was her biggest sale during her tenure with the company. Her father would be thrilled. Before she could pick up the phone, the man of the hour was standing in her office doorway looking handsome as ever except he was missing something; that devastating smile he wore like a well-fitted pair of skinny jeans.

Joshua Jamison Sr., at sixty, is one of Philadelphia's most prominent leaders. His company, Jamison Telecommunication, started out as an alternative telephone service for small Black-owned businesses that could not pay the exuberant prices of the top telephone companies. Joshua Sr. was blessed to have a father that was a hard worker. He not only paid for him to attend and graduate from Howard University, but he also gave him the needed capital to start his business before he passed away ten years ago. Like his father, Joshua Sr. had a reputation of being fair and honest. His professionalism attracted several top-notch clients of every nationality. Fifteen years since its inception, Jamison Telecommunications has made Joshua Jamison, Sr. one of Philadelphia's richest men. His company reached #75 on *Forbes* top 100 family-owned and operated companies last year.

"Joelle, I'm tired of you showing up late every day. I called you for an impromptu meeting at 8:45 a.m. before your 9:00 a.m. meeting with the Mott Hotel. Stella tried covering for you, but I knew you hadn't gotten in yet."

"But, Daddy, I got the—"

"I don't care what you got. At Jamison Telecommunications, we pride ourselves on being efficient and prompt. I expect a strong sense of commitment and professionalism from every employee working within this organization. Therefore, I cannot have my Director of the Telephone Division being late every day. Even if she is my own flesh and blood. Joelle you are facing a professional death by getting a reputation of being tardy. I can you give us your "A" game once you get to work, but your lateness is starting to discredit all of your accomplishments, including the newly acquired two-million-dollar deal with the Mott Hotel."

Despite being an heiress, Joelle never took advantage of her status. In fact, all of the Jamison children worked hard in one capacity of the family empire. Both Joshua Jr., and Jonah were heads of the cable division. Even Johanna managed to find her niche working with the up-coming wireless division. The only one not in the loop and often referred to as the black sheep of the family was Jacob. Joelle listened to her father's rantings, waiting patiently for an opportunity to make him eat his words. Joelle was used to her father riding her about being late, but today he seemed extra agitated. While Joelle was trying to figure out where all the hostility was coming from, she thought her ears were playing a trick on her. She thought she heard him say that he was demoting her, but that couldn't be right.

"You're kidding me, Dad. In case you didn't know, I just scored the Mott Hotel as a client. Now, I'll accept your apology and we can forget this conversation and I can get back to work."

Joshua Sr.'s altered look in no way suggested that he was offering an apology. In fact, Joelle didn't know whether she should be running to Macy's to get their newest Gucci bag for her success, or running for cover. He hadn't looked at her like that since she came home at 5:00 a.m. prom night. Her other brothers were already out of the house, so all eyes were on Joelle. She spent a month talking her parents into letting her go on prom. After all, the Jack and Jill ball was supposed to be its equivalent. And yet, Joelle begged her parents to allow her to go to the prom a week after the ball so she could laugh it up with her high school friends.

She even told her mother she would wear the same gown, but Johanna wouldn't have her daughter in the same dress at two different affairs even if different people were in attendance. It just wasn't done. Once they decided to allow her to go, Johanna immediately purchased her a dress a little less pricey than the one used for the ball, but just as extravagant. Joelle didn't take a date. Instead, she and her homegirls went together. There was a little alcohol involved, which was the culprit for her arriving home late or should I say early the next morning to an extremely annoyed father who was about to call her three brothers who would have been there in less than twenty-four hours.

"Joelle, I am aware of your success with the Mott Hotel, but that doesn't excuse the fact that you have been late more times than anyone in this company. I cannot and will not tolerate this. With that being said, you will get your commission for scoring the Mott Hotel, but effective immediately you will be demoted to a sales representative. Jonah will oversee your department for two months, at which time you are expected to be here by 8:30 a.m. sharp every day in order for me to consider giving you our old position back. You will report to the second floor where you will find your cubicle."

With that, Joshua Sr. walked out of Joelle's office leaving her with a look of utter disbelief on her face. Afterall, Joelle took her job as Director of the Telephone Division very seriously. Her job was like her premature baby, born to soon. With all the tender loving care she constantly gave it, she made it a success. Despite all of the hard work, Joelle's lateness was the one problem that had become her Achilles' heel.

Had she not just had her hair relaxed and he nails recently manicured, she may have been tempted to pull it out a strand or two at a time. At that moment, she wished she could distance herself from her family like Jacob had done.

After graduating college, Jacob moved to Houston, Texas. With a portion of the inheritance his father set aside from, he opened a comedy club and restaurant called AMUSE! Once a month, he hosted a teen night to deter crime and drug use amongst teens. He was seen as a leader in a community that desperately needed someone to give a damn about its youth. Jacob was not afraid to take on the so-called thugs that felt they were to be feared and revered for being what Jacob called a "punk." Jacob was never worried about his safety, but he was always aware of his surroundings. He definitely didn't go looking for trouble, but he wasn't about to let others keep him from being a beacon to the young boys and girls in his crime-ridden community who deserved to grow up healthy and happy.

It was at one of these events he met his wife, Eve. Neither one was looking for love that night. Eve was a reporter assigned to cover the event for the local newspaper after her boss got wind that Jacob came from a wealthy family in Philadelphia. He wanted Eve to see if Jacob was the real deal or if he was a fraud that would leave the community at the first sign of trouble. Eve was surprised when he agreed to an interview with her during the event. He asked his assistant to take over and escorted her to his office for some privacy. Jacob was unaware until later in the relationship that Eve was mesmerized by Jacob the moment she saw him.

Jacob in turn was immediately taken in by Eve the moment she walked through the door. He expected a member from the local press to attend, but he was not expecting someone as breathtaking as Eve. She was curvy and had features that looked Caribbean. Jacob knew that God had created this particular Eve for him. He vowed that night that she would be his wife. He spent two hours talking with her about his passion for working with young people and owning his own business. He even told her about his family. Two months later, they were married. The Jamison clan ascended on Texas to attend the low-key wedding despite numerous objections from Johanna. She felt that a grand and lavish wedding with at least 500 guests was required for the first Jamison child to wed.

However, Jacob and Eve stuck to their guns and got the intimate wedding they wanted. Joelle remembered that Johanna didn't speak to the two until after the I Dos were exchanged. Her father politely pointed out to her mother that it was their lives, dreams, and future and not hers. Despite this initial difference of opinion between the two women, Eve was soon welcomed into the family with open arms by Johanna. Eve would check in on the family in Philadelphia on a weekly basis. She would share what projects she and Jacob were working on with Johanna and have sister talk with Joelle on a regular basis.

The happy couple were approaching their fifth anniversary when tragedy struck. Joelle could still remember the phone call she received from her oldest brother relaying the events that led up to Eve's homicide. The family tried to be supportive, but Jacob refused their calls and pushed them away almost immediately after the funeral. It was discovered shortly after that Jacob blamed himself for Eve's death. Apparently, he failed to take down a burglar in their home before he was able to get off three shots. Two bullets ricocheted off the wall into nearby furniture. The final shot struck Eve in the chest. Her life was cut short over a few dollars. Jacob's routine was to bring all the money collected that day home for deposit the following day. He must have been watched and followed home. If only he had just given the guy the money. Eve would still be alive.

Despite the family's assurance that it wasn't his fault, he has carried this burden for the last two years. He stopped most communication with the family except for a monthly phone call to his mother reassuring her that he was okay. However, he did not let them know where he was staying. Her two brothers went to Texas to find him, but had little success. Jacob was like a ghost with the ability to disappear into thin air. His brothers left Texas feeling a little defeated, but they would not be deterred from their mission of supporting their brother through the grief process when he was ready for their support. Since Jacob was the lost son, Joshua Sr. put a lot of effort into taking an active role in his other children's lives. He was determined to make them strong, successful, and sensible adults. He kept two eyes on the boys and his third eye was fixed on Joelle. This was one of the reasons he gave them all top positions in Jamison Telecommunications.

A solitary tear slid down Joelle's face. The fact that he was somewhere isolated from their close-knit family was heartbreaking. He had taken the road of the prodigal son, except he left the riches and fanfare behind with his family's prayer that he would find his way back home. Joelle couldn't remember the last time he called her. Jonah stated that he had spoken to him briefly on Jacob's birthday. Being the two middle children, they shared a bond that the others couldn't touch.

Determined, she quickly wiped away the tear and walked back to her office with a sense of urgency. Stella was nowhere to be found and neither was the tote bag with the kitten. Stella was quite efficient, but so was Joelle. She would prove her father wrong and get her position back come hell or high water.

Chapter 4

"I asked if you received your calling?" James stated.

Xavier took a mug from the shelf and poured himself a hot cup of coffee. Sitting in his father's church study was not exactly where he thought he would share his news. Xavier still couldn't figure out how to tell his father about the bookstore, but because his work was almost completed, he couldn't keep it a secret for much longer. Xavier knew it was wrong to keep this important decision from James, particularly since James had been more than a father, he was Xavier's confidant. However, with all the rumors about Xeria, Xavier didn't want to add to his father's list of worries.

Speculations arose that Xeria was dating a married man, but no one in the family directly spoke on the subject with Xeria for fear that she would deny it and then distance herself from the family. More importantly, they knew that gossip was a powerful thing and they refused to speak life to it within the family. But X knew that James was getting tired of the rumors. The gentleman in question supposedly was a prominent member of Living Vine. But without a mother, James only had himself to blame for not sitting Xeria down and having the same discussion he had with Xavier and Xavian about male and female relationships. James had quoted scriptures about not coveting another man's wife, so he assumed Xeria knew that the same applied to married men. This was an assumption that might not only cost the Lawerence family the loss of Xeria, but the loss of James's beloved Living Vine if James didn't get to the bottom of it prayerfully and peacefully.

Xavier knew that he couldn't keep sidestepping the issue, though. He would have to tell his father about his investment, and there was no better time than the present. To sell the point with his father, he could tell him he would have Xeria help out in the store to earn an income and so he could keep an eye on her.

"Dad, I'm afraid it's not the calling you were hoping for. Have a seat, Dad."

James's look of concern made it imperative for Xavier to make haste. But before he could speak, James interrupted him.

"Don't tell me you got the calling to be a father? If so, I expect you to man up and take care of your responsibilities. And—"

"Whoa, Dad!" Xavier held up his hands. "I didn't get anyone pregnant. But... I am about to give birth."

"I'm confused, Son, you're going to have to help your old man out."

"It's like this, Dad. I was led to open a Christian bookstore."

James scratched his head and let out a sigh of relief. "That's not what I expected to hear, Son."

James put his head down and clasped his hands together. Xavier couldn't tell if his father was going to pray or what, but he was becoming increasingly nervous while he waited. He really wanted his father's approval. But he knew his father wanted him to follow in his and his brother's footsteps, so Xavier looked to see if he could read his father's expression.

"So, are you upset?"

"I was pushing you to become the next pastor of Living Vine, but God has led you in another direction. I am concerned that you have limited experience in owning a business, but it's your life."

Xavier fought back tears at only gaining his father's partial approval. He knew he was taking a big chance by opening up a bookstore devoted to Christian literature and paraphernalia. He wasn't sure if it would work, but he would exercise his faith over fear. He hoped he would be able to prove his father wrong and pay him back the money he loaned him two years ago when he got his degree in Divinity. A degree he wasn't sure he was going to use in the way his father would have wanted. Xavier quickly pushed the thought away and then immediately filled James in on all the specifics.

"It sounds like a real nice store, Son," James stated after hearing his son speak so passionately about his "baby."

"Hey, old man, would you like to see the place?"

Xavier was hoping that if his dad saw the place, he would feel more confident about the bookstore. He was also hoping his dad would spend time working in the store and even consider a lecture series on various topics. Xavier respected his dad in and outside of the pulpit. He had wisdom that Xavier was sure his customers could benefit from. He had to convince his father that his calling for now was the bookstore as he was not sure how long he could manage the bookstore without his father's full approval.

"I would love to, Son. But first I have a meeting with the Deacon board. Can I meet you there in an hour?"

"Sure, you have the address, so I'll see you there."

Both men grabbed their jackets and headed out to their vehicles. Philadelphia weather could be so deceiving. The temperature in his truck read 78 degrees, but it was much cooler this summer's day. Xavier started his truck and headed towards When the Saints Go Marchin' In bookstore.

The first thing on the list to do once he got to the store was to call the telephone company. He recently read an article about Jamison Communications. After doing his own research, he was impressed with the professionalism this Black-owned family business offered. He decided to have them handle his store's telephone system and cable services. He just hoped they were accessible and would give him the personal one-on-one customer service the bigger companies could not. Xavier turned up his radio and found himself singing the classic song "Dance with My Father" by Luther Vandross. As he was singing, a single tear slid down his face. While he felt extremely blessed to have a supportive father like James, he wished his mother was alive so she could see the bookstore as well.

He wished she was there to walk him down the aisle when the time came and hold his firstborn child. Xavier wiped away the tears and continued on his drive to the bookstore. He turned up the music and then a thought hit him. In the past, Xavier has had trouble dealing with overbearing sales people. He was praying that whomever his sales representative, he or she would listen to his needs and be professional. The bible speaks about living in peace whenever possible. He subscribed to that wholeheartedly, except when he felt he was being disregarded and /or disrespected.

Chapter 5

The elevator opened and Joelle stepped out. It was exactly 8:30 a.m. Joelle was for the first time in nine months on time. When she surveyed her surroundings, she realized that this was the first time she actually had been on the second floor also. She usually bypassed it and went straight to her office on the fourth floor. Jamison Telecommunications was housed in a five-story building in the Bryn Mawr section of the city.

Joshua Jamison Sr. started the company on one floor in an industrial building in Manayunk. As the accounts started coming in and his business started expanding, he needed more space. With the help of a small business loan and the money his father gave him, he purchased the factory-style building and renovated it into the state-of-the-art office building that it is today. Working in the company, Joelle watched as the physical structure modernized over time.

Joelle knew that her new office space wouldn't be like her luxurious office on the fourth floor, but she knew it would be comfortable and chic. Joelle would report directly to Jonah, who in turn would oversee her department until she earned her former position back. Joelle was confident that Jonah would treat all of her clients with respect and professionalism. She was a little concerned about Mott Hotel, given that they just landed the account. That meant she would have to do all she could do to regain her former position back as soon as possible. She knew her father didn't want to cause too much confusion for the staff who were used to taking orders from Joelle. Also, she knew he was trying to teach her an important lesson on punctuality and accountability.

She walked down the line of chic cubicles not knowing which one belonged to her. Some had high desks to help those who couldn't sit for too long and others had large exercise balls that employees could bounce on for light exercise. To her surprise, her name was on an office door with a new plate that read Joelle Jamison, Senior Sales Representative. She smirked as she walked into the office to find Jonah behind the desk. Jonah was the spitting image of their father, Joshua Jamison, Sr.; like his father, he received quite a few gasps from females in and outside of the office. Jonah's best quality was his smile. He had a dimple on his right cheek that would make a woman weak in the knees. At that moment,

Joelle remember a time when he was just her annoying older brother and not the handsome snack she overheard women discuss while in the company's restroom.

"So how do you like your office, Sis?"

"I like my office on the fourth floor better." Joelle tossed her briefcase on the desk.

"Oh, come on. I had to twist Dad's arm to get you this office. The least you could do is say thank you."

Jonah got up and positioned himself in front of an absolutely irritated Joelle.

"Thank you, but you and I know that Dad has gone too far with this demonstration." Joelle stepped around Jonah and sat in her chair behind the desk. At least it was comfortable.

"I'm not taking sides, Joelle. All I know is that I need you to hold up to the agreement by being here on time so you can have your department back."

Joelle knew why he was adamant about wanting her to step her game up. She knew the extra time in Joelle's department would take time away from his extracurricular activities. Everybody knew that Jonah worked hard, but she suspected he played just as hard.

"Don't worry, I got it covered. I was on time today."

Joelle could tell he was tuning her out. He had a faraway look in his eyes. She had to snap him back into reality. She turned up the volume a little in her voice.

"One day at a time built Rome," Joelle stated as she glanced at the manila folder on her desk. It read "When the Saints Go Marchin' In bookstore" on the corner label.

"That's a new client. The owner of the store is named Xavier Lawerence. He called earlier and I told him that our top sales representative would be calling him back later today."

Jonah moved towards the door to make a hasty exit.

"Look Joelle, call him to set up a meeting ASAP because he expects to have his bookstore open in two weeks. He needs his phones set up by next week."

Jonah walked out and shut the door behind him before Joelle could protest. Joelle wasn't used to dealing with small accounts like this. After the two-million-dollar Mott deal, Joelle couldn't see herself working with a Ma & Pa business. Unfortunately, she didn't have a choice in the matter.

"Well, Mr. Lawerence, let's get this party started. Fifty-nine days and counting."

Chapter 6

It had been two hours since X made the call to Jamison Telecommunications. In that time, his father had come for a quick tour of the place and then left. X showed James where the café would be. He planned on selling coffee, tea, and pastries. When he had more time to research and was making a profit, he would consult a local Black-owned bakery to get fresh cakes and pies delivered daily. X also had a burn bar where patrons could burn their favorite music from various artists on a CD, for a reasonable fee of course. X knew most people liked one or two songs off an album and downloaded those two instead of purchasing the entire CD.

The burn bar would cater to those types of patrons. Even though most people downloaded their songs from Amazon or Apple iTunes, he knew that some people still had CD players in their cars. Those people who didn't want to pay for SIRIUS XM or for wireless, would appreciate the burn bar. X wasn't looking to make a lot of money off it; he just wanted to provide the option for those old-school saints who liked having a product in their hand instead of on an app or as a download. The rest of the store housed numerous translations of the Bible, study Bibles, uplifting spiritual books by some of today's best preachers, and sections devoted to teenagers and children.

X had been pushing his father to write a book. He knew James could rival such authors as T.D. Jakes and Creflo Dollar. Once written and then published, he would put his father's book in the front display case. Until then, he could gain a following by hosting lectures in the bookstore. He would also set up book signings and.... Xavier had to pump his brakes. He first needed to get his father on board with writing the book. He couldn't see that his story of being a single man raising three young children was extraordinary and needed to be told. He was putting the cart before the horse considering his father hadn't given writing a book a second thought with all the other responsibilities on his plate. He still had to find a spot for the children's section affectionately known as Little Saints' Corner. He would have children's Bibles, games, and weekly story time. Maybe he could get Xeria to spearhead the kids activities including the story time. X glanced at his watch again.

"Why hasn't someone called me back yet? I'm starting to think that it was a bad idea to go with a smaller company."

X reached for his cell phone and started dialing. Before he could dial the next number, someone was on the other end of the line.

"Hello, hello, is someone there?" X could hear what sounded like a mixture of a soft and sultry female voice.

"Yes. Is this Mr. Lawerence?"

"Yes, it is. How can I help you?"

"Mr. Lawerence, this is Ms. Jamison from Jamison Telecommunications. I was calling about your impending account with us."

X started imagining the face that matched the voice on the other end of the phone. She sounded like she was strong and confident, but there also was a softness in her voice that reminded X a lot of his late mother. Jamiah Lawerence was an example of a Proverbs 31 woman. She epitomized a wife of noble character. X remembered how she would open their home to all the children in his father's congregation and the community the family lived in.

Along with sounding strong and confident, he sensed that she was professional. She told him about the options and packages she thought would work best for his individual business. She was not trying to sell him the most expensive package, but the one that would suit his needs. This is what he was hoping for in regards to being able to work with his assigned representative. Someone not trying to nickel and dime him and sell him accessories he didn't need. He was determined to not be taken advantage of when it came to the bookstore. He had to prove to his father that he had made the right decision.

"So, if you don't have any more questions, I can connect you to our service department and they can set up a time to install the system."

X realized that he wanted to speak with her more. In fact, he knew he had to meet her in person to connect the voice with the rest of her. Although looks were important, he was drawn to something else about her. Something so powerful that he didn't want to be transferred or handled by any other person but her. It didn't matter what she looked like, X was drawn to her spirit and energy. He could tell she was passionate about her job. She had nothing but good things to say about her company and the owner. She didn't mention her relationship to the owner. He assumed she was a niece or cousin. After all, there was no way the president's daughter would be handling a small account like his. That suited him fine. He figured that would mean more drama if he was dealing with the heiress of a multimillion-dollar company. She was probably beautiful with a touch of arrogance that comes with money.

In his past, X had dated several beautiful women in and outside of church with and without money. He preferred outside of the church because church breakups were always sticky. He had taken a hiatus from dating for two months and had been celibate for six months. X came close to getting married two years ago to an attractive woman by the name of Jenny. Jenny was a successful banker. She was sweet and on paper and had all the qualities he looked for in a woman. The only thing that she didn't have was Christ. Jenny didn't believe in "God" per se. She claimed to be spiritual, but she did not attend any church service, nor did X ever see her pray to any God except the all mighty dollar. X thought that she would come around after attending a few church services with him. He was hopeful that God would touch her and fill her with his love just as he did for him.

Unfortunately, she never did let God completely into her heart. Despite that, after two years, he proposed even though his family objected. The heart wanted what it wanted and X wanted her. Of course she accepted before he could put the ring on her finger. X had given in to a lot of her demands about the wedding. But X realized they were not meant to be when she said she preferred to have an outdoor wedding instead of a church one and that she wanted some of the references to God taken out of the ceremony so as not to offend any of her worldly family and friends.

X didn't know the exact quote about if you deny God on earth He will deny you in Heaven, but he knew better than to get involved with someone who denied God; that could be his downfall.

X asked a few more questions to keep her on the phone. He was trying to find out as much as possible about her. As she spoke, he tried to imagine what she looked like. He imagined her skin tone and what she physically looked like. Although he was usually attracted to fit women, he really didn't care what she looked like as he found her conversation intriguing. While he was usually not so aggressive when it came to meeting a woman in person. He preferred to have a few conversations over the phone because women were less guarded over the phone. Also, he didn't want the physical to get in the way of discovering who she really was, the good, the bad, and everything in between.

CHAPTER 7

Joelle had just given a great pitch over the phone and was about to transfer Mr. Lawerence to the service department when he said something that caught her off guard.

Did he say he wanted me to come out to meet him at the store for a one-on-one conversation? Joelle thought.

"Excuse me, Mr. Lawerence our service department will do a fine job of installing the telephone lines. If you have any questions afterwards, please call."

Joelle listened as Mr. Lawerence explained how his business required one-on-one service and how he needed to meet with her personally. Her mind said *no*, but out of her mouth came yes. She didn't know why; it just came out. It was something about his voice that sounded urgent. He needed to meet with her, and she wanted to know why.

"Okay, Mr. Lawerence, so we'll meet at 4:00 p.m. tomorrow. I will have the service department come out the following morning to set up the equipment."

Joelle hung up the phone. She had a tingling sensation in the pit of her stomach. She chalked it up to being hungry. She grabbed her newest Gucci bag and headed for the door. She locked the door and turned around and came face-to-face with Joshua Sr.

"Hello. Joelle, how is everything going?"

Joelle hadn't spoken to her father since the transition.

He was true to his word by depositing her healthy commission check into her bank account, but that didn't make up for her demotion.

"Father" was all Joelle could manage.

"Jonah told me that you have been on time every day. Good start on getting your former position back."

Joelle smiled despite wanting to scream. She figured that her father knew demoting her would hurt her personally and professionally. What she did not know was that he had been approached by several supervisory level personnel about the favoritism being shown to the members of the Jamison family while others were being written up for coming in at the same time as those of his family members. To the point where some employees threatened to sue if they were fired.

"Thank you, Father. Is that all? I'm leaving for lunch and I'll be back in exactly an hour as specified in the employee handbook." Joelle stared her father directly in the eyes.

"Don't get cute. I'm still your father and I will not be disrespected," Joshua Sr. stated.

"From 9:00 a.m. to 5:00 p.m., you are my employer. Now, if you will excuse me, it's my lunch and time is slipping away. Goodbye, Mr. Jamison." With that, Joelle walked away. She didn't mean to be rude or disrespectful but she wanted to make a point. Joelle fished her phone from her handbag and dialed her childhood friend's number to see if she wanted to have lunch with her.

"Hey, girl. You want to grab lunch at Matches?"

"Sorry, girl, I'm swamped with work. Can we meet up for dinner tomorrow?"

"I have a 4:00 p.m. meeting with a client, but it should be over by 4:30 p.m. at the latest," Joelle stated, breathless as she hustled across the street to make the light.

"Oh, is this the first client since your demotion?" Justine chuckled.

"Yeah, I had the deal wrapped up over the phone when he threw me a curveball by asking to meet with me face-to-face."

"What? Does he sound sexy?" Justine asked inquisitively.

Joelle had to choose her words carefully before she answered. She knew Justine would have her married off to Mr. Lawerence if she told her about the smoothness in his voice.

"He sounds professional and he's client and that's all that matters. Bye, girl!"

Joelle quickly hung up to avoid encouraging Justine. She opted to go to the café off Broad Street to ensure she would be back on time. She saw a couple of upscale eateries that looked like they provided expedited services. She spotted a café sandwiched between a CD store and a store that was being renovated. She read the name of the store. It was called When the Saints Go Marchin' In. This was Mr. Lawerence's bookstore. Joelle could feel a sense of peace as she gazed at the store. Before she knew it, her feet were gravitating towards the store. She crept up to the window feeling like a stalker. She wanted to try to get a glimpse of the man with the urgency in the voice. She wasn't even sure if he was there, but she was drawn to this store this very moment. She cupped her hands around her eyes and peeked through the glass. She couldn't quite make out anything until she saw a pair of gray eyes peering back at her.

Chapter 8

X looked up as he saw a woman approaching his store. She had a glow on her face that reminded him of someone he knew. Her hair was pulled up into a nice neat bun with strands falling around her beautifully sculpted face. Not knowing who this woman was, X felt a tingling sensation in his stomach. Any other time he would have thought it was hunger pains, but not this time. It was crazy, but he felt a connection to this mystery woman.

She walked to the main break front window and started looking in. Not wanting to miss the opportunity to get a closer look, X moved over to the window. He didn't mean to startle her when he looked her in her brownish almond-shaped eyes. X quickly withdrew from the window and held his breath. It was almost like he looked into her soul. X always had the ability to read people at first glance. In fact, his family always teased him about his gift of discernment. It was X who picked up on the shiftiness of her sister Xeria's boyfriend. He could never look X in the eye when they were talking. At a family function, Xeria walked in with puffy eyes as if she had been crying. Immediately X's eyes shifted towards Deval searching for some type of information as to why his baby sister was upset.

Deval acted as if nothing was wrong and proceeded to go into the kitchen. X walked over to Xeria and questioned her about her appearance. Before her tears could hit the floor, X was all over Deval. Deval tried defending himself but was no match for X's agility and precision with inflecting body blows. Xavian and James had to pull X from beating Deval within an inch of his life. James ushered Deval out of the house while Xavian held X. James didn't know quite what was going on, but he knew enough to pray before he did something he would later possibly regret. Afterwards, Xeria reluctantly told her father and brothers about Deval's abusive patterns. All three were in a rage. If it wasn't for prayer, all three would have went over and literally laid hands on him.

X shared his concerns with Xeria, but she told the three men in her life that they were being too overprotective. At James's urging, X and Xavian let it go. Later, X was more upset with himself and not Xeria for not following his instincts. X couldn't get Xeria's shattered, hopeless look out of his mind long after Xavian's wife Julia escorted her into the bathroom to freshen up. After that day, he vowed that he would not neglect the gift that God gave him and follow his instincts. X saw the strange woman withdraw from the window. He had to move quickly so as not to let her get away. X rushed and opened the front door just as she was about to walk away.

"Can I help you?" X stated. She looked up at him with startled eyes.

"I didn't mean to scare you. I saw you looking in and I wanted to know if you needed something."

X tried to remain calm, but her presence was exciting him in a non-sexual way. It was almost like he met her before in another lifetime.

"I was just admiring your store" was all Joelle could manage to say.

"Not much to admire yet, but thank you. It should be up and running within the next two weeks." X had to concentrate on the words that were coming out her mouth instead the exquisiteness of her mouth.

"I wish you a lot of success. It's nice to see a Black-owned business in this neighborhood."

X could tell she was nervous and about to bolt. He couldn't let her. "I can offer you a tour."

"No, that won't be necessary. I have to go. Have a great day."

With that, she ran across the street. As X watched, he felt pain in his rib. It was like it was ripped from his side. He had to find out who she was somehow, someway or he would not feel complete.

Chapter 9

Joelle felt that her face was flushed as she quickly made her way through the parked cars to get as far away from Mr. Lawerence as possible. It was something about him that felt familiar, but it put her in a frenzy as well. She didn't know how she would handle meeting with him tomorrow. She couldn't face him again so soon. His very scent was overwhelming and masculine. He was everything she looked for in a man. He was tall and his golden brown complexion was flawless. He sported a clean cut goatee that was accentuated by his close-cropped curly black hair. Joelle's family had always teased her about marrying a light-skinned man, but she blew their comments off. Mr. Lawerence was in fact the improbable man of her dreams. Joelle had to find a replacement to take her place at their meeting tomorrow.

Maybe she could convince her coworker Ron to meet with Mr. Lawerence. Just as she was about to dial his extension, she remembered that she would need to run the idea by her brother first. As the director, he would be the one to assign the accounts. No doubt since Jonah was temporarily in charge, he would want to be just as involved.

"Jonah here."

"Jonah it's me. Look, I have a meeting with Mr. Lawerence tomorrow to discuss his account and—"

"Yes, he's a new client and I am hopeful that it will be profitable for both our companies.

Are you ready?"

"That's why I'm calling. I think Ron should take the account."

"Why?"

"I just can't do it."

Joelle sensed that Jonah was not buying her back-out plan, but she stuck with it anyway.

"Well, unless you can give me a good reason Joelle—"

"Umm...."

"It's yours. Bye, Sis."

Joelle looked at the phone. She couldn't believe he hung up on her. A part of her wanted to dial him back and give him a piece of her mind for hanging up on her, but she knew it would be of no use. Once Jonah made up his mind, a person needed a damn good reason to change it. Unfortunately, Joelle's reason was far from good.

I mean, what can I say?

"Umm... yeah, Jonah, I can't meet with him because I'm smitten with him. Or, he took my breath away. No, better yet, he's too damn sexy for me to put together a sensible sentence let alone a proposal together."

Joelle would have to find a way to be professional, after all she was trying to get her former status back at the company. She had to prove to her father that this move intended to teach her a lesson about being on time was a temporary one. Joelle headed back to her office in a frenzy. Her mind was racing. As she approached her office, she knew the first call she had to make would be to Justine. Justine would know how to handle the situation. Unlike Joelle, Justine works around and interacts with all types of fine brothers all day long.

She is the proud owner of a sports bar and grill. Justine inherited the business from her uncle upon his death. Justine's first inclination was to sell the bar. It didn't fit into her plans of being a financial planner at a prestigious firm downtown. After completing her graduate degree, she was confident the offers would start pouring in. After two months of returned resumes and no call backs, Justine was at her wits end and about to be homeless. Joelle was not about to let her girl be homeless.

Joelle suggested that she considered running the bar. With no other prospects, Justine used what little money she had and with a small business loan from Joelle, she did minor renovating and opened the doors to Uncle Joe's a month later. Since then, Uncle Joe's had become one of Philly's top spots and was voted the best bar and grill in its first full fiscal year. Justine has acquired a fabulous chef and first-class staff to support her in her quest for success. She even improved the menu to include comfort foods and high-end cuisine. Justine is definitely doing the darn thing.

Just as Joelle stepped back into her office, she recognized the figure sitting smugly in her chair. Jonah couldn't help but smirk as he watched his sister fumble to catch her falling briefcase.

"What are you doing here? Why are you sitting at my desk?"

"I was worried. It's not like you to relinquish a client... so what's up?"

Joelle had to be careful how she answered her brother. She loved him but she knew she had to use a lot of tact with him. He, after all, was the closest out of the four Jamison children to their father and was known for having loose lips.

"I was concerned with the time factor. That's all."

"How so?"

"Look he's a new client and I pondered if I could give him the attention he needs while

dealing with my other clients."

"Give me a break, Joelle, I have seen you effectively juggle two to three million-dollar accounts at one time. You can't bologna style me."

Joelle hadn't heard him say that since they were kids. It was a no-no in the Jamison household to use profanity. As a result, the Jamison children came up with other sayings to replace the words, but they said them with the same intensity. Banana Split was another way of saying bullshit. Joelle noticed that Jonah was not saying anything. She assumed that he had asked her a question, but she didn't hear him.

"What did you say?"

"I asked you the real reason you wanted to be pulled from the Lawerence account?"

"Okay, okay, It's not a big deal. I can do it. I'll just have to reshuffle a few things and it will be fine."

Joelle made her way over to the desk and with her hand she shoved her brother out of her chair. He got up slowly and walked around the front of her desk to face his sister. Joelle knew she couldn't fool him by trying to play it off, but she thought she would give it a try. He smiled and started making his retreat. Joelle modestly accepted this victory knowing that the battle was far from over. Jonah would find another opportunity to bring this discussion up. She hoped he wouldn't do it in front of their father. Joelle grabbed the phone to call Justine before some other storm found its way in her path.

Chapter 10

Xavier finished unpacking the boxes delivered shortly after his encounter with the lovely stranger, aka, the Peeping Tom. He had tried his best to busy himself so as not to think about her, but to no avail. Xavier felt that this wasn't the last time he would gaze upon her. He learned not to lean on his own understanding, but to wait on the Lord. They would meet again and she would be his Ruth to her Boaz.

"Wow, where did that thought come from?"

X hadn't realized that those last thoughts were vocal until he heard a coughing noise behind him.

"I think you should open this store ASAP so you have someone other than yourself to talk to, Big Brother."

Xeria giggled. X was so caught up in his own thoughts that he didn't hear his sister come in. He had recently given his father and both siblings a key to the store for emergency purposes. Xeria's busy schedule made her the last person he expected to actually use the key.

"Hey, Sis. I didn't hear you come in."

"I could tell. I was in the neighborhood so I thought I would check out the progress you were making on your store."

Xavier knew she was not telling the whole truth. Xeria rarely visited, especially on a weekday. X wasn't sure if this was a good time to bring up asking Xeria if she wanted a job working at the store or not. He knew she was preoccupied with other matters at the moment, particularly Deval. But X wouldn't say anything. He knew it was best to let her get it out in her own time.

Xeria hadn't really opened up about what happened between her and Deval. Despite their father's grim looks, Xeria was tight lipped.

"Do you want a tour?" X asked.

He wanted to keep her there as long as possible in hopes she would loosen up just enough for him to inquire about her life.

"No thanks, another time. I have to run to the store to get a few things for a dinner party

I'm having."

"I don't remember getting an invite with all the particulars."

"It's just me and a couple of friends you don't know," Xeria stated flatly.

"So I'm not good enough to hang out with you and your friends. Wait, I know most of

your friends and they love me."

Xeria started gathering her belongings, leaving X looking on, waiting for her to say something.

"It's nothing, Big Brother. You're invited to my next get-together, I promise."

"I'm going to hold you to it. So how is everything?" X listened patiently.

"Great. But listen I gotta go."

Xeria kissed X on the cheek and ran out the back door before he could even say goodbye. His sister couldn't go on much longer avoiding the discussion on what was bothering her, especially it if was about the alleged relationship between her and the married man at his father's church. How she managed to be involved in two toxic relationships, X didn't know. But the next time X was alone with his sister, he would make it a point to push her about what's really going on. X made his way over to inspect where the phone lines would be installed. He wanted to make sure everything was ready for his appointment to-morrow with the representative from Jamison Telecommunications. X just realized that he was intrigued by two women at the same time. Tomorrow he would meet the seductive-sounding woman at Jamison Telecommunications and someday hopefully meet the peeper that was looking through his window earlier today. The thought of both women brought both a smile and a grimace to X at the same time. Being intrigued with two women could only lead to heartache and a hard fall.

Chapter 11

Joelle woke up early the next morning ready to take on the world. Yesterday she was in a frenzy trying to figure out what she was going to do about her meeting with Xavier Lawerence. After not being let off the hook by Jonah, she inhaled and slowly exhaled and then came to her senses. She remembered who she is.

I am Joelle Jamison, the Director of the Telephone Division at Jamison Tele-communications. I am no amateur that can be swayed by a handsome face. I am a professional, damn it, she thought. Her father raised her to be a strong and confident woman. She would act in a professional way and take charge of the meeting today no matter how fine Mr. Lawerence looked today. If yesterday was an example of how good he could look in jeans and a tank shirt, she had no doubt he would look just as sensational in professional attire. Joelle looked at the clock and decided that she had better get a move on it if she wanted to be on time for work. Joelle started the shower and jumped in. Since she was early, she decided to take advantage of the showerheads' massage functions. When she stepped out of the shower feeling all refreshed and revived, she looked at the clock. To her astonishment, It read 8:15 a.m.

"Get the heck out of here. I couldn't have been in the shower for that long." Joelle quickly dried off. She would have to change her course of action. Even if she got dressed in twenty minutes, there was no way she would get to work on time. She had to think of a plan. She dialed Jonah's extension at the office.

"What's up, Sis? I hope you are not calling to tell me that you're going to be late?"

"Oh ye of little faith. I was just calling to let you know that I had to move my afternoon appointment to the morning. I'll be in after lunch."

Joelle hoped that Jonah wouldn't see past her slight fabrication. She knew she had a tell and that Jonah usually could spot when she was lying. He figured out her tell the night of the prom when she came in at 5:00 a.m. Joelle tried to sneak in without being noticed. She carefully took off her heels, lifted her Donna Karen Dress, and tiptoed up the stairs. She had almost made it to her room when out popped Jonah from the bathroom. He was home from college for the weekend. She put her finger to her lips and motioned for Jonah to come into her room. She knew that he would have a problem with her coming in late, but he would cover for her since she was his sister. When he looked like he was about to hit the roof, she knew that she would have to have to come up with a great lie to appease him. She started off by telling him that the limousine broke down on the way home. She went on to tell him that the breakdown affected the power, which included the phone. As the words came out of her mouth, she could feel her eye twitch.

That reaction lead to a fast-and-furious line of interrogative questions about what time it broke down, where it broke down, and what happened to her date. Joelle felt corned; almost like how Jinx feels when he is corralled into a cat carrier for a routine visit to the vet. Jonah knew that she was lying, but to prevent him from becoming even more disputatious, Joelle decided to tell him the truth in order to get him out of the room before their parents woke. That ship had sailed when Joshua Sr. entered her room with his eyebrows raised. Jonah tried to save his sister from their father's vehement tongue lashing. Unfortunately, it was to no avail. Jonah exited the room, carefully closing the door behind him. Both he and his mother listened at the door as Joshua Sr. tore into Joelle.

Both jumped back from the door when he came storming out after grounding Joelle for what sounded like an eternity. Johanna brushed past her infuriated husband into Joelle's room to comfort her daughter. Since that time, the entire family was made aware of Joelle's tell to help keep her in check and on the up and up. Since then, Joelle has worked on trying to keep her tell from ratting her out. Luckily, Joelle was not face-to-face with Jonah, thus the possibility of her being able to pull off this lie would prove to be victorious.

"Is it the Lawerence account?" Jonah asked.

Jeez, how could Jonah remember her client log with so many other things on his plate. It was like he was a machine when it came to the job. This character trait has taken him far in the business world. If anything ever happened to her father, God forbid, Jonah would do an exceptional job of running the business. The only thing standing in his way would be their eldest brother Joshua Jr. Joshua Jr. works just as hard as Jonah and since he is the oldest, he is likely to take over the empire upon Joshua Sr.'s death. Joelle hated thinking about a future without her father, despite how upset she was with him at the moment.

"I just left your office. How did you call him to reschedule the appointment if the folder is on your desk?"

Joelle didn't know whether to be more annoyed by his lack of trust or the fact that he was in her office. Especially since she thought she locked her door when she left yesterday. She decided to distract him by focusing on his unauthorized entry in her office.

"Wait, what were you doing in my office? Just because you supervise my department

does not mean you have the right to break and enter into my private space. I mean really, Jonah. I might have expected this from Joshua Jr., or Dad, but not from you. I have to go. I'll see you after lunch."

Joelle hung up before Jonah could protest. She knew that her semi-tantrum would buy her some time. However, she would have to come up with a creative fabrication about how she was able to reschedule the appointment with Mr. Lawerence with no contact information in less than five hours. But, that was the least of her worries. She had to find a way to get Mr. Lawerence's number, and then pray he would be able to meet with her this morning instead of this afternoon. Joelle decided to call in the big guns. She called Joshua Jr. She knew he would help her if she really sounded desperate and played the sweet little sister card. Just as everyone knew Joelle's tell, everyone also knew that Joshua Jr.'s tell was that he had a soft spot for Joelle. In all of five minutes, she was able to get her brother on the phone and ask him to retrieve the much needed contact information from her office. He said he would call her back in ten minutes. Joelle smiled and went into her room to get dressed for her meeting with Mr. Wonderful. Oops, she meant Mr. Lawerence. She would have to look professional and alluring at the same time. She was going to knock his socks off. Joelle, wondered what had gotten into her. Sure he was sexy as heck, but he was a potential client. She had to get her mind right and focused on the objective at hand; score that account and continue on her quest to get her former job back.

Chapter 12

Xavier ended the call with a puzzled look on his face. It was strange receiving a call from a Mr. Jonah Jamison Telecommunications confirming that the appointment with Ms. Jamison was rescheduled from 4:00 p.m. to 10:00 a.m. At first, X was not sure what Mr. Jamison was referring to seeing as how he hadn't spoken to Ms. Jamison about moving up the appointment. He decided to play along sensing that this was some sort of sibling thing that she would definitely have to explain when they met at 10:00 a.m.

He quickly got dressed. Before jumping in the car, he checked himself out in the mirror to make sure he had his swagger going on. He had exactly ten minutes to get to the bookstore before her arrival. He decided to make a quick stop at the corner bakery to pick up some chocolate cheesecake pastries and two cups of coffee. He figured Ms. Jamison would scarcely have enough time to cook or purchase breakfast. Also, he figured it would be a good diversion while she thought of a good excuse for moving up the appointment unbeknownst to him. He promised he would not give her too much of a hard time given her apparent need to prove something to her brother.

He knew what it was like to prove something to a sibling. After all, he had been trying all his life to prove to his older brother, Xavian that he was not the slacker he thought. Xavian was behind X's bookstore venture halfheartedly. X knew his brother thought that this was just a fly-by-night plan. In the past, X had dabbled with many vocations before finding out what God's purpose for him was. During his discovery period, he had spent a lot of other people's money. Most of the funding was provided by his father, but he did manage to get a few hundred dollars out of Xavian when he wanted to sell T-shirts.

The business almost worked, but Xavier overspent his hand. He had too much inventory and not enough enthusiastic paying customers. As a result, the business went down the drain, Xavian was out the money, and Xavier was left with 2000 "Have you Seen my Babe Ruth" and "Searching for my Boaz" T-shirts. He figured that Bible readers would know what the sayings meant and buy into it. No such luck. Xavier just finished paying Xavian off last year. He knew Xavian still kept a close eye on X's business ventures. This time, his brother would see that the bookstore was God ordained similar to his calling as the pastor of his New Life Baptist Church. X was so caught up in his thoughts that he barely heard his cell phone ringing. He recognized the number. It was Ms. Jamison.

Joelle was grateful her brother Joshua Jr. was able to get the contact information on Mr. Lawerence in a timely manner. Joshua Jr. mentioned that his mission was briefly interrupted by their brother Jonah. Apparently, Jonah wanted to know why he was in their baby's sister office, particularly since he had not been down to visit Joelle since her demotion. Jonah knew that Joshua Jr. would not provide him with any information about his activity in her office. Joelle knew Jonah would question her later as to the reason why Joshua Jr. was allowed in her office without her permission and he was not.

"Hello, Ms. Jamison. I was expecting your phone call." X couldn't help but smile as he wondered what expression Ms. Jamison had on her face at this very moment.

"Mr. Lawerence. How did you know it was me? I don't remember giving you my cell phone number." Joelle managed to get this quick statement out before a small drop of perspiration slid down the right side of her face.

"I obtained your number from Mr. Jonah Jamison this morning. He confirmed that our appointment was moved up to 10:00 a.m. Although I was totally oblivious to the appointment change, I decided to play along. I asked for your number with the intention of recognizing it when you called to catch you off guard just as your brother caught me off guard."

"Since you are aware of the change in plans, can we discuss this more when I get to your bookstore? I should be there by 10:00 a.m. as I am only ten minutes away," Joelle stated.

"Wait, how did you know I was available to move up the appointment?"

"I'll see you in ten minutes, Mr. Lawerence."

Xavier hung up the phone with a smirk on his face. He was excited about finally being able to put a face to the voice. X could hardly contain his excitement. He unlocked the front, de-activated the alarm and placed the morning delicacies he purchased on the counter. That feeling in the pit of his stomach was back. He didn't know what it was about her, but he was drawn to her. Her only red flag seemed to be with time. She never addressed his question about his availability. He was very particular about time.

Breathe, Joelle, Joelle thought to herself as she approached the Christian bookstore. She hoped that Mr. Lawerence wasn't watching her, but there was nothing she could do about it if he was. She flung her hair over her shoulder, secured her briefcase, and strutted across the street.

X couldn't believe his eyes. Could it really be that the voice on the other end of the phone at Jamison Telecommunications was the Peeping Tom? If that had been the case, why hadn't she told him that yesterday? Could it be that she was just as taken by him as he was by her? X slowly walked over to the door so as not to appear so anxious. His heart was beating a mile a minute.

Breathe, Xaviar.

Just as Joelle reached for the door, someone on the other side opened it. It was then that she came face-to-face with the most attractive male specimen. Mr. Lawerence was dressed in a white, collared dress shirt with a navy blue tailored jacket. His attire was polished off with a pair of dark navy jeans and black loafers. Despite his physical appearance, it was his essence that was most intoxicating to Joelle. He reached out to her. Joelle didn't know if she should take his hand or not. She quickly regained her composure and shook his hand with a mixture of softness and assertiveness.

"Ms. Lawerence. It's nice to meet you. But haven't we met before? X couldn't help himself. He didn't want to make her nervous, but he did want to see how she would handle herself in stressful situations should something arise while working on his account.

Joelle knew what he was doing. She had found herself in stressful situations before; although not with someone as sexy as Mr. Lawerence. He was testing her. Little did he know, she was more than up to the test. Joelle thought back to her conversation that almost ended the Mott acquisition.

"Two million dollars is a bit pricey for two phones per bedroom and less than 50 additional phones for the rest of the hotel," Mr. Mott stated arrogantly. *"Is your father around? I think he would be willing to play around a little more with these figures."*

Joelle had no intention of having her father join in on the meeting. Mr. Mott was trying to play hardball, but little did he know, Joelle was a master at the game.

"Mr. Mott, I'm afraid my father is otherwise engaged. But I can assure you of the authenticity of this offer. It is a fair price and non-negotiable. So if that is all, I'll have my secretary show you out." Before Joelle could stand, Mr. Mott was signing his John Hancock on the dotted line. Joelle's insides had been doing summersaults. Gracefully she extended her hand to close the deal with Mr. Mott, while assuring him that he would be extremely impressed with their services. Unfortunately, Joelle's victory was short-lived with the father's abrupt announcement about her demotion.

CHAPTER 13

"Mr. Lawerence, it's nice to meet you. And, yes, I think we have met. You look vaguely familiar."

Joelle's smile all but melted Xavier's heart. He was taken away by her startling appearance from head to toe. Before he was able to focus on her attire, he took in her scent. It was like all of his senses came alive with one whiff of her. She wore a soft, sweet fragrance that transported him back to another time and place. A time when his mother was reading to him after one of his hay fever episodes. It wasn't quite the same, but it smelled similar. It made him feel safe. Xavier then took in her choice of attire. She wore a matching two piece pale yellow suit. The hem of her skirt played with her midthigh and her hips added something extra that made Xavier's mouth almost water. She wore flesh-color stocking and a pair of dark yellow pumps to finish off her ensemble. Careful not to fall under this woman's spell, X accepted her hand ever so gently. It was soft to the touch.

"So why didn't you tell me you were Ms. Jamison during your visit yesterday?" X stated.

Joelle tried to think of a witty response that would prove to be a little elusive and coy, but nothing came to mind. This annoyed her since she was normally able to keep other people on their toes. This was crazy. This man was able to take her off her square, so to speak. Joelle knew she had to get it together before she lost this account; possible ruining her chances of getting back her former position at the company.

"I noticed that you were watching me, which put me and my company at a dis-advantaged. I opted to keep my identity secret until our meeting today to give my company more credibility in the eyes of a potential client such as yourself. Our job is our handle our clients' needs with accuracy and proficiency. In order for me to do that, I felt it necessary to retreat from your store anonymously so as not to cause any misrepresentation on my part. Please accept my utmost apology for stopping by yesterday unannounced. I was in the neighborhood hoping to get a quick bite to eat when I saw your store." Joelle didn't know where that came from, but she thought that she nailed that response. In fact, she knew she nailed it.

Xavier heard the words as they eloquently dripped from Ms. Jamison's lips, but he was not listening. He was so engrossed with her luscious lips that he couldn't think straight. She wore a pale shade of shimmering pink lip gloss. He imagined kissing her softly at first. Something about her suggested to him that she would like it that way. She would want to be tasted and enjoyed. It was in her eyes. Afterwards, he would deepen the kiss. Before the fantasy could go any further, Xavier realized that there was a looming silence in the air. He knew he would have to say something or he might scare her off, when instead he wanted to drag her to the shower and make her scream in a more intimate way.

"I assure you, Ms. Jamison, thus far I am impressed with the way your company has been handling me." Xavier managed to keep a straight face, barely.

Joelle was amused by that comment; however, she was not going to give Mr. Jamison the satisfaction of knowing it. If he thought that his smooth, confident demeanor would throw her off, he didn't know the Joelle that has handled more powerful men than him. It was game on from here on out, despite the words that were coming out of his moist, firm lips. At that point, Joelle didn't want a battle of wits, but a battle of lips. She internally shook herself to focus on the task at hand of securing this account and getting out of this man's presence as soon as possible.

"Okay, shall we get down to business, Mr. Lawerence? I'm sure you have other matters to attend to, as do I, this afternoon."

Two hours later, they were able to hammer out all of the details of the contract. Mr. Lawerence was more than happy with the multiline phone system that would be worked throughout the store. Joelle felt like she nailed it. She stood up ready to extend her hand to Mr. Lawerence and make a hasty retreat. When he took her hand, she felt a tingle shoot through her body. She wondered if he felt the same thing.

Xavier felt a jolt of what he could only describe as electricity when she placed her hand in his. From that moment on, he knew that he wanted to get to know Ms. Jamison on a deeper, more personal level. Even though their meeting was coming to an end soon, he would definitely see her soon. Even if that meant he would have to dismantle the entire multiline phone system before it was even completely installed.

CHAPTER 14

Joelle woke up in a cold sweat. She just had the most exhilarating, erotic dream about the sexy shop keeper she met with yesterday. Part of her wanted to immediately go back to sleep to relive every hot moment, but she knew she needed to get up and head to work. She needed to put all of this foolishness behind her and focus on getting her old job back.

She stretched and then headed towards the shower. She set the knob on the appropriate setting and began her descent into the shower. But before she could get in, she heard the telephone ringing from the bedroom. She glanced at the clock. It was 6:15 a.m. Who in the world could be calling her this early in the morning. At first she thought it might be her father. Since their last blowup, he had been trying to get back in her good graces. No such luck.

She has been dodging his calls left and right. At some point she knew he would pay a visit when his feelings were starting to get hurt. Despite the tough exterior, he was a softie, especially when it came to his family. After the prom fiasco, Joelle refused to talk to him for weeks. Even Joelle's mom could not coax her into forgiving him until Joelle was good and ready. Eventually, the two made nice and their relationship got back to normal. The only other person it could be was her estranged brother Jacob.

Jacob rarely called; however, when he did, it was often early in the morning. She hadn't spoken to Jacob in months, so she would welcome a call from him. She knew his wedding anniversary was coming up soon and she worried how he would cope. She slid across the bed and reached for the phone.

"Hello."

"Hello beautiful. I was just calling to make sure you were up. Wouldn't want you to be

late for work."

Joelle was both excited and irked at the same time when she realized that it was Mr. Lawerence on the other end of the line. She was excited because she was just thinking about him. Despite what she thought earlier about the business of getting back to business, she did enjoy fantasizing about what it would be like to wake up in those strong arms after an amazing roll in the hay. She was irked because how dare he assume that she was not mature enough to get to work on time. He didn't know how hard she worked when she did eventually arrive to her office. He didn't know that she was usually the last person to leave except for the cleaning crew. She placed her social life, what little one she had, on the back burner in order to ensure she was on top of her game. More importantly, he really didn't know her well enough to make a judgment call right or wrong about her. He was not family or one of her closest friends that knew about her tardiness problem. He helped her out yesterday, but that was just one incident.

"Mr. Lawerence...? Good Morning. How did you get my home number?"

Xavier could not believe he really called her. He toyed with the idea all night after he managed to snag her home number from her office. It was easier than he thought, which was awesome and alarming. He told the receptionist that he was a new client of hers and that he needed to get in contact with her immediately. At first she was a little apprehensive. After all, she didn't know him from Adam. It took some time, but he was able to convince her that he was Joelle's client and that his motives were genuine and authentic. Part of his need to speak with her was professional, yet most of it was for personal reasons. The reason being his attraction towards her. He decided to give her a wake-up call in the morning. The abrupt meeting change yesterday that was orchestrated by a call from her brother, led Xavier to believe that Joelle must have a problem with lateness. He didn't know to what extent, however, he knew that he needed to make sure his future "wife" was always on her game.

Wife? Whoa, Xavier, calm down. You just met this woman.

Xavier didn't know where this notion came from. All he knew was that it felt right. He did not dismiss that the existence of the Holy Spirit was working in this situation. As a result, Xavier decided to go with it and give her a call. He hoped she would not be upset with him or the receptionist when he told her she gave him her number.

"Don't be angry, but I called your office and told the young lady that I needed to get in touch with you immediately."

"The receptionists at Jamison Telecommunication are very thorough. I can't believe you were able to get the number out of her," stated Joelle.

"You are correct. It took a great deal of professional jargon to get her to not even hang up on me. I explained that I was a new client and told her that I needed to contact you immediately or the deal would be off.

"Oh, Mr. Lawerence, you don't seem like the type that makes threats."

"Normally I am not, but in this case I had to go there."

Joelle could have spent more time grilling him, but she decided that it would be pointless banter. Afterall, she was excited he called. However, she would have a talk with Nancy when she got to work about not giving out her number to anyone for any reason. If the person threatened to pull their account, then so be it.

"To answer your question, yes I am up and getting ready for work. In fact, I have the shower running as we speak." Those words brought vivid images to Xavier. Before he could fully let the fantasy develop, she asked him another question. "Why would you assume I needed a wake-up call from you?"

Joelle really wanted to ask him why he cared. Afterall, they had only met yesterday and her personal life was something that he should not even concern himself with. And yet, she felt something magical and special. She felt like he was taking care of her. She hadn't felt like that in such a long time. She had to admit that it felt good. Some men are intimidated by an independent woman. Last time Joelle checked, women wanted to be interdependent with their mate which meant both embraced their independence but incorporated it into something magical where each took care of each other interdependently.

"Well, yesterday's meeting switch gave me an inkling that you may struggle a little with being on time for things. If I'm off the mark... well, please accept my apology."

Xavier feared that he had made the wrong decision in calling her. She could hang up on him and then assign him to another sales representative at her company. She could virtually exit his life just as quickly as she entered it. He decided to make haste and end the conversation in the event that she was pissed about his forwardness. At least he would keep the business connection intact, thus giving him the opportunity to approach her through another door.

"I guess I was wrong, Ms. Jamison. I won't take up any more of your time."

Joelle sensed that he was trying to end the conversation. What she didn't know was why. She was enjoying his seductive voice. However, with one look at the clock, she knew she needed to end the conversation if she was going to be on time for work. She hung up after a sultry goodbye, but she hoped that they could finish their conversation some other time. The ball would be in his court, though. Afterall, she is an old-fashioned girl with hopes of being pursued.

Chapter 15

Xavier ended the phone call feeling hopeful. He could tell that even though he made the first move by calling her about something other than business, he would have to follow up with some way to converse with Ms. Jamison soon. Something in his spirit could tell that she was an old fashion girl looking to be wooed and pursued. The only question was how he would pull it off. Before he could continue with this line of thought, his phone rang.

"Hello." No answer. "Hello. Is there someone there?" Still nothing. Just as Xavier was about to hang up before he said something he would regret, he heard faint sniffles. Someone was definitely on the line. The only question was who. "I can hear you crying. Who is this?"

X was more concerned than annoyed at this point about the unknown caller on the phone. He checked his phone prior to answering it and it said restricted. X rarely answered unknown calls. His emotions were getting the best of him in that he hoped it was Joelle calling him back.

"Xavier, it's me Xeria. Please help me."

Xavier's heart dropped. Why was his baby sister calling him crying? In his heart, he knew only one person could make her cry like that—Deval. X's mind started racing. Had he hurt her physically or mentally? It didn't matter. Deval would pay regardless. Xavier got so caught up on seeking revenge, he almost forgot to get the particulars about what happened and where she was. He questioned her as gently as he could, but with a sense of urgency in the event he lost the call. He quickly wrote down the address she gave him and rushed out the door.

On the way over, he wondered if he should contact the other two men in Xeria's life; his father and brother. He didn't know what he was walking into or how he would find her. For now it was best for him to handle it on his own. He pulled up to the address and jumped out of his car with quickness. He was standing in front of what looked like a twin four-bedroom home in the West Philadelphia section of the city. The shades were down as he approached the screen door. He opened it and pounded on the door until the porch light came on. X found it strange that the person on the other side of the door would put on the light since it was in the am. The door slowly opened. From behind the door stood a scrawny woman with a jacked-up weave that was bright red. As he took her all in, he could see the needle tracks in her arms. She was definitely a junkie. The question was what was she doing in this house.

X surveyed the living room that housed a dirty two-piece sofa set and a stained wooden table in the middle of the room. X saw tracts stationed on the table that had information about overcoming drug abuse and a bible. The tracts looked written on and some were crumbled up as if someone read them and wanted to toss them in the trash, but instead tossed them on the table. X felt as if he was in some sort of sanctuary despite the pieces of debris on stained carpet. This left X officially perplexed? Why would his sister be in a place with drug addicts? Before he could say anything, Xeria stepped from behind the woman. X wasn't sure how he missed her.

Her beautiful face was darkened by what appeared to be someone's fist in several places. She had a black bruise on the left side of her face. X's anger rose as he surveyed the rest of her body. Her clothes were in disarray. He got all the way down to her feet when he noticed that she was not wearing any shoes. What the heck happened to her? Before he could question her, a tear slid down her face. At that moment, all he could do was reach for her. She fell into his arms and softly sobbed. He held her for what seemed like an eternity, but in actuality it was only a few moments. She turned around and thanked the girl that answered the door for her assistance. X couldn't imagine why Xeria would be thanking this woman since it looked like she couldn't even help herself.

However, X was taught that only God can judge. So he thanked her and wrapped his arms around his baby sister and led her to his car. He opened the door and helped her in. As she was sitting down in the front seat, she winced a little. X suspected that she may have had broken ribs. Without one word to her, he drove her to the ER. He thought she would protest, but she didn't. She allowed him to open the door and the ER staff brought a wheelchair for her. As they wheeled her back, X felt that he needed to notify his father and brother about the situation. He knew whoever did this to Xeria would need more than prayer to save him from the wrath that would be brought down on him by the Lawerence Clan.

CHAPTER 16

Joelle could not concentrate on anything at work. All she could think about was Mr. Lawerence and his lovely wake-up call. She thought about giving him a call to check on the phone system, but who was she trying to fool. She just wanted to hear his voice. Joelle had to admit to herself that she was attracted to this man. She could tell that the feelings were mutual. She decided to give him a call. She dialed the new store number. It rang and rang and rang. She hung up feeling a little stupid.

Even though he seemed attracted to her, he may be in a relationship or in something close to it. How naïve of her to think that she may be his only interest. Afterall, this man was fine. This was crazy. She decided to get back to the business of working. She had several calls to make before the day was out. Ten minutes later, Joelle needed a break. She looked at the clock. It was almost lunchtime. What better time to call her "bestie" and get out of the office for a quick bite to eat. She dialed Justine's number at the restaurant. After confirming that they would meet up at the hospital, Joelle got her belongings together and headed out the door.

Even though Justine served the best food at her establishment, the two loved the meatloaf served for lunch on Wednesdays at the hospital. Joelle discovered the fine cuisine when she was waiting for her father after a same-day surgery procedure a year ago. She told Justine about it and they were both hooked. Justine even tried to persuade the cook to jump ship to work for her. Unfortunately, he could not be bought, so to speak. He said it was his calling to bring delightful, delectable, delicacies to ailing people in the hospital that normally would get the traditional "Hospital Food." With that being said, both women decided that they would have to come to his "house" when they felt like they needed a real down-home comfort meal.

Joelle stepped out of her office building and headed down Market Street. As she approached the hospital, she saw a familiar face. She could only see a side view, but she could recognize X's masculine stature from miles away. Her face lit up as she approached the unsuspecting gentleman. She wondered what brought him to the hospital on a workday when he should be getting ready for his grand opening. Just when she was within speaking distance, she saw a woman approach him. Joelle stopped and turned around slightly. She then moved over to a nearby tree.

She felt like a teenage girl not wanting to be seen by the object of her juvenile crush. This was foolish. Why should she hide from him? What would it matter if he saw her? She stepped from behind the tree and saw X hugging the most-captivating woman. He then took her hand and they walked through the emergency entrance. She was so caught up in what she was witnessing that she did not realize that her phone was vibrating. It was Justine.

"Hey, girl. Where are you?"

"I'm outside."

"Well, girl... get your butt in here. I'm sitting at our table waiting for you."

Joelle wanted to tell her she was on her way. She wouldn't let seeing X with another woman who may have been his sister, cousin, colleague, or even significant other stop her from the mouthwatering meatloaf she had waited all day for. They were not in any type of relationship, except a work-related one. Why should she care who he was with.

"I can't come in. I need you to come out."

"Are you kidding me? What's wrong?"

Justine could tell there was something wrong with her girl. She had no idea what it could be though. They had just spoken thirty minutes before and she was "down with the get down" when it came to devouring meatloaf at the hospital.

"I'll tell you when you meet me back at your restaurant."

Joelle turned around and started walking towards Justine's grill. Several thoughts ran across her mind. She did not realize how much this thing with Mr. Lawerence had affected her. She did not have visions of marriage or anything, but she did envision him in her life. She didn't know how she would handle seeing him again, or what she would say if he called her with a work-related problem. Lucky enough she wouldn't have to see him again if she chose not to. She knew that Justine would have the right words to make the situation all better. She just hoped she could get through the conversation without shedding any tears. She quickened her pace to get the restaurant.

After Xavier filled his sister-in-law in on Xeria's condition, he left her in the waiting room with his father and brother to make a phone call. His heart was breaking. He and Xeria had a close relationship since her birth and their mom's premature death. Until recently, she would tell him just about everything that was going on in her life. With the entrance of Deval, came the exit of their close-knit, tell-all relationship. X wanted to make sense of it, but for some reason he couldn't wrap his head around it. He needed to talk to Joelle. He would keep his sister's confidence by not sharing what was happening to her; heck, he didn't quite understand it himself, but he just needed to hear her voice before he exploded.

CHAPTER 17

Joelle was already waiting in their reserved booth when Justine entered the restaurant. Justine looked beautiful as usual. She really didn't have a conventional style, she just knew what looked good on her and she worked it. Joelle often wished she could be as care-free as her friend. Unfortunately with a mother like hers, fashion was key to getting and keeping clients in the telecommunication industry that so happened to be dominated primarily by those of the male persuasion.

Joelle did not inherit her mother's frame, which was okay with her. Joelle loved that she was shaped with more substance on the bottom than the top. She had a small waist and ample, C-sized breasts. But it was her hips that seemed to attract suitors. Joelle, although not a fitness fanatic, did manage to get in three workouts a week at the gym to keep toned. Although her focus was not presently on attracting a mate, she knew the importance of having a good physique and keeping her auburn, highlighted waist-length tresses pressed and well oiled. Joelle was often told she resembled the famous R&B singer Aliyah.

Even when Joelle expressed to her mother that it was somewhat of an insult for her to suggest that the only way she got her high profile clients was because of her appearance instead of her educational merits, her mother smiled, nodded, and then insisted that she apply an extra coat of lip gloss before each meeting. No matter how old, or how good she was at her job, Joelle knew her mother word never see her as a competent, hard-working woman with the same strong business skills inherited from her father just like her brothers.

Justine exhaustedly fell into the seat across from Joelle. Before she could say a word, she got the attention of one of her employees and held up her hand motioning for two drinks to be brought over to her table. Her exceptional staff were well aware that that particular hand motion meant that they needed something stronger than their usual drinks. Justine knew that this conversation required Appletini.

"So what's up? You sounded so devastated on the phone." Justine took a sip of her martini and waited patiently for Joelle to fess up.

Before Justine could inquire any further, she saw a tear slide down her bestie's face. *What the hell happened?* she thought. Because Justine was an only child,

Joelle was the closest thing she had to a sister. Justine, typically not a fighter, would cut someone if need be for Joelle. If she couldn't fight them, she would call 911 and tell such a tale that they would fight for her. She remembered how much Joelle helped her when she needed it. Justine was determined to find out what was wrong with Joelle. If need be, she would threaten to call one of her brothers. In the past, that threat would get her to spill everything.

Justine knew that Joelle adored her brothers, but both Joelle and Justine thought that their overprotectiveness had completely hindered and prevented her finding her Mr. Right. Justine knew that if anyone hurt Joelle, that person would have hell to pay when they came in contact with her brothers. The Jamison brothers' reputation for being over-the-top when it came to their sister was communicated throughout the telecommunications industry. Even though Jacob was going through it and currently estranged from the family, he would be on the first plane home if he caught wind of someone hurting his little sister. Because of that, Joelle was cautious about sharing matters of the heart with her brothers.

Justine was envious of their bond, being an only child. She wished there was someone in her corner that would "Ride or Die" for her. That was one of the top reasons Justine was only interested in dating men from large families. Since she didn't have brothers and sisters of her own, she wanted a man that did so she could have brothers and sisters-in law she could claim as her family. That is also why she was grateful for her friendship with Joelle and her family.

"I saw him with another woman," Joelle stated in between sobs.

"You saw who with a woman?"

"Mr. Lawerence."

"Ohhh." Justine couldn't understand why Joelle was upset. Joelle stated that it was only business with this man. Justine thought otherwise because she could hear the enthusiasm in her voice when she spoke about this man. But she didn't think he had this much of an effect on her that she would actually be shedding tears over him.

"I know that it's crazy, Justine, and that I told you that it's professional, but he called me at home and we talked about things that were not work related."

"Hold up. How did he get your private number?"

"My secretary gave it to him when he told her he had an emergency with the phone system in his bookstore," Joelle managed to explain between sobs and a running nose.

Joelle hadn't realized that her sobs had become long and hard, making it difficult for her to catch her breath. Before she knew it, she was hyperventilating. The last thing she heard was Justine instructing her to breathe. She put her head between her legs before everything went black.

CHAPTER 18

It had been two days since X last spoke to Joelle. He was tempted to call her yesterday, yet he was a little apprehensive. He said he needed to hear her voice for a sense of calm, but he never got a chance to call her since the doctor told the family Xeria's injuries required her to be admitted into the hospital. At that point, things became very confusing and chaotic in the family. Despite pressure from their father, Xavian, and X, Xeria was not talking about what transpired between her and Deval or what landed her in what could only described as a recovery house for drug addicts.

What X didn't know was that Xeria knew all too well what would happen to Deval or anyone else that hurt her. He was unaware that she was protecting the men in her family. By not telling them what happened to her to prevent them from getting incarcerated for Deval's murder, she was frustrating them all as well. All X wanted to do was protect his baby sister, and if that meant putting Deval in the same hospital as Xeria, then so be it. X's thoughts were interrupted by the ringing of a cell phone. Deep down he prayed it was Joelle.

"Hey, Daddy." X only called his father Daddy when he needed him to be in the protective role and not the ministerial role.

"What's the matter, Son?"

"Just worried about Xeria."

"I just talked to her. She's still not talking about what happened to her."

X expected as much. When they were kids, Xeria was able to keep a secret for days. The same could not be said for X and/or Xavian. They would give up the tapes, so to speak, with just one look from their father. Xeria on the other hand managed to keep cat hidden in her room under her bed for two weeks before it was discovered by X. She begged him not to tell, but he did not honor the code between siblings. He quickly ran and got Xavian. Xavian looking for brownie points with their father quickly called their father and exposed her once well-kept secret. To everyone's surprise, James allowed them to keep the cat. The only thing that he insisted on was that they look after the cat with little supervision from him. This put a lot of pressure on Xavian. He was not too happy about having another thing to look after. With the passing of their mother, Xavian was primarily left to taking care of his siblings when their father was busy at the church, writing sermons, or visiting the sick and shut-in.

X knew that Xavian loved his siblings, but he and Xeria were a handful when they were children. X actually felt bad for how he and his sister treated Xavian. They had denied him a childhood because he was always in bad-cop mode. He was the one to tell them. "No, No, No." During those times X would long for the days prior to his mother's death. X was plagued with issues surrounding hay fever. It would keep him up a night. Jamiah would come in with a warm washcloth and place it on X's forehead and tell him tales about David and Goliath and Samson and the Philistines. X was easily engaged in the vivid picture his mother would paint about biblical heroes. At the end of the tale, she would remove the homemade remedy cloth, which of course, had no medical value, and kiss him on his forehead. Those memories of his mother always made X feel a little better about life and the possibility of finding someone as special as his mother.

"You know your sister won't tell us anything until she is good and ready," James stated with a somewhat saddened tone.

"I'll go by to see her tomorrow, Dad." X wanted to give Xeria her space, but he knew that if he gave her too much time, she would not open up until it was too late, and he would be damned if he let Deval hurt her in the meantime. X got up early and went to the bookstore to retrieve his messages. With the grand opening a week away, he had to make sure there weren't any messages that required his immediate attention. Normally he would be excited and counting down 'til the big day, but with all of the drama going on with Xeria, he was exhausted. He grabbed a pencil to write down the messages. He listened to them all feeling a little disappointed. Even though he hadn't called Joelle, deep down he wished she had called him. X couldn't understand how she managed to get under his skin so quickly. The feelings that he had were so intense that if his mind wasn't wrapped up on Xeria, it would definitely be all wrapped in Ms. Jamison. He vowed that as soon as he got back from the hospital, he would call her.

He knew that someone as charming and charismatic as Joelle wouldn't be on the market much longer, that was if she was on it at all. During their early morning conversation, she seemed to enjoy the flirtatious banter, but who was he kidding? Joelle was a very beautiful woman. She could have had that conversation with just about any guy. Yet, he knew that they shared something special that he was willing to fight for as soon as this business with Xeria was stabilized. X grabbed the mail that he piled up on the counter and headed out to the hospital. The sooner he dealt with Xeria's situation, the sooner he could focus on Joelle.

When X got to the hospital, he entered what he thought was his sister's room. He had a cup of coffee in his hand in preparation for spending a few hours with his sister. He knew if she wasn't ready to talk, he would nurse his piping hot cup of Hazelnut coffee for the duration of his stay as he never wanted to leave her even when she told him to go. As he was entering, he dropped his parking ticket. He bent to pick it up, and as he was placing it in his back pocket, he looked up and recognized her immediately even though her head was slightly turned, facing the window.

She turned her head slowly the exact moment she felt the presence of someone entering the room. His heart just about broke when he saw what appeared to be dried tears in her eyes. Before he knew it, he was beside her with her hands in his. As soon as Joelle looked in his eyes, tears started falling uncontrollably. She didn't know why she was crying in front of this fine, fine man. She could only attribute it to the fact that she saw what appeared to be empathy and concern in his eyes. Outside of her brothers and father, she couldn't remember any man looking at her in such a way. Her past relationships has left her feeling empty and sure that love was not in the cards for her. She was the one that would put her all into the relationships until she began thinking like a man. She decided that she would only give out what she was getting.

If the man only wanted a sexual relationship, she would be the one who decided when and where. Because of her financial situation, most men were willing to deal with her terms. They were willing to wait for her feminine pleasures believing that eventually she would be seduced into sleeping with them. To their dismay, this never happened. Joelle was very picky about who she slept with. She would only sleep with someone that was her husband or definitely on his way to being her husband. She only went as far as kissing and some fondling, but she never felt the push to go all the way. Deep down she knew it wasn't fair to the guy, but she was upfront about her terms. She told them that in her past relationships she never actually went through with the deed because there was something that often prevented her.

Deep down she knew it was the Holy Spirit whispering to her to, "wait, child," or "he ain't the one, child." Eventually they would get the picture and step off. Joelle decided to hold off on romance to prevent hurt feelings. Also, she didn't want to get into a situation where the man she was with didn't care about her terms and was willing to take her treasure because he couldn't pull back. She would hate for some female to tease one of her brothers in that way, especially her brother Jonah. He had an addictive personality. Once he gets involved in something, he has a hard time letting go. However, no one could put a finger on his recent preoccupation. Joelle and her siblings noticed that he was being elusive around the office, which meant some new person or preoccupation had got his full attention and was slowly forming into and addiction. Even though he had the added responsibility of running her department, he still managed to vanish for several hours and reappear during important meetings or conference calls. Joelle was so caught up in her thoughts that she hadn't realized that she had been staring at X for some time. She tried to turn away, but she couldn't.

When she started to open up her mouth, he placed his fingers on her lips almost as if he wanted her to save her strength by not wasting her breath. As touching as this was, she had to know what brought him here to her. She believed in fate, but this was a little too good to be true. Joelle woke up in the hospital after passing out at Justine's grill. She was told it was a combination of low blood sugar from not eating and anxiety. Joelle hadn't realize how much work she was putting in in this new role. Because she was no longer dealing with large accounts, she has many small ones that took up more time than the bigger ones partly because she couldn't delegate the smaller tasks to a subordinate. She was always on the go putting out fires, which left little time for her to eat. The anxiety was more about making sure she was juggling everything in order to prove to her old man she deserved her old job back sooner than later.

Mentally she was okay, so she thought, but physically her body couldn't take the strain. So, that day at Justine's place her body said enough and it went down. And now she was here. She needed to find out why he was here. The last time she saw him, he was hugging a beautiful woman at the very hospital she currently resided at. She had to find out and fast to avoid any additional stress.

X just wanted to look at Joelle. He didn't want her to talk. He just wanted to admire her. It was then that he knew without a shadow of a doubt that she would not only share his bed, but also his life. Some people would call it wishful thinking, but he knew better. He knew it was the Holy Spirit whispering, "*She's your Eve, my child*" and "*Bone of my bone; flesh of my flesh.*" He could put it off not longer. He had to know what brought her here. He prayed it was not the result of someone hurting her. If indeed someone had, he would have hell to pay. If he was willing to go to jail for Xeria, he was damn sure willing and ready to not only go to jail, but give his last breath for Joelle.

"What happened? Did someone cause you harm?" X tried to stay calm, but he was anxious to know what was going on with Joelle.

Joelle didn't know what to say. Could she really tell him that she was admitted to the hospital due to an anxiety attack over numerous things, including him. Her mind kept racing to the mysterious woman. Who was she? Was she his significant other or a casual fling? She couldn't bare risking her heart if he was indeed even remotely involved with someone. Right as she was about to respond to his question, she noticed a stranger peering in her room.

"Can I help you?" Joelle stated a little apprehensively.

X quickly turned around to see who she was referring to and found his brother Xavian standing there. No doubt Xavian must have seen him on his way to visiting their sister. She was in a similar-style room to their sister's two doors down. In fact, they were very similar, which is how he had ended up in Joelle's room.

"I think he is here for me," X stated. He placed Joelle's hand back down on the bed by her side.

He didn't even realize that he was holding her hand. X got up and walked over to his brother. Joelle watched the two men exchange a few words. As the conversation was progressing, Joelle could see that something was wrong. She saw that the other man was looking away, as if was intentionally trying to avoid direct eye contact with X. She saw a strong resemblance between the two men. She assumed that it was his brother. What she didn't know was why they both were in the hospital. She assumed it had something to do with the girl she saw X speaking with. Just when she thought her curiosity was going to get the better of her, X finished his conversation with the gentleman and returned to her side.

"I'm sorry, but I have to go. The person I came to visit is being discharged and I have to take her home." X tried to remain calm because he thought it was too soon for her to be released. He felt that she needed more time to heal and that she would be safer in the hospital away from Deval. He was determined to have the conversation about her working at his store as soon as possible. He was surprised his father hadn't brought it up, but he knew it was on his father's mind.

"Can I call you later?" X held his breath while he waited for her answer. He wasn't sure what she would say.

Joelle didn't know what to do. She desperately wanted him to call her, but she still didn't know who the other woman was. Everything she knew about X suggested that he was a stand-up kind of guy. She decided that she wanted to speak with him later. She would find out if he was involved or not. And if he was, she was willing to walk away despite the feelings she'd developed for him over this brief time period. At least that is what she told her heart.

"I'll be waiting for your call." X did something Joelle did not expect. He smiled. Not only did he smiles with his mouth; he smiled with his eyes. Joelle could only smile back. X kissed Joelle on the inside of her wrist in such a way that was not only sensual, but it was endearing as well.

<h1 style="text-align:center">CHAPTER 19</h1>

Joelle was released from the hospital at six that evening. Despite her objections, she was accompanied home by every member of her family except Jacob. She didn't know how they managed it, but they all knew about the doctor's diagnosis of acute anxiety within thirty minutes of her being admitted. She knew she had only Justine to blame. She would call her later and give her an earful.

First, she needed to reassure her parents and siblings that she was okay enough to be left alone for the evening. She knew her father felt somewhat responsible for her situation. Even after she tried reassuring him. She thought that would be enough for him and the rest of the family to take a hint and show themselves out. No such luck. While her mother spent time picking up clothing that Joelle has left lying around, her father and brothers were busying helping themselves to leftovers from her favorite restaurant. She didn't want to admit it, but she was anticipating X's call despite not knowing how to broach the subject of whether or not he was involved in a relationship. Joelle was so caught up in her thoughts that she did not even see her brother standing in her doorway watching her.

"A penny for your thoughts, Sis."

Joelle didn't know whether or not she should share with Jonah or not. He was definitely not known to keep a secret. However, she needed to get the opinion of a man on how a man thought. She decided to bend the truth a little bit with Jonah. Since Justine got her into this situation, she decided she would use Justine as her decoy.

"Justine has man problem and I am very worried about her." Joelle wanted to see if he would bite. He did. After Joelle explained the situation substituting Justine's name for hers, she waited for his response. She didn't know if he would see the glass as half-empty or half-full. If the glass was half-empty, he would probably advise Justine to leave well enough alone. If he was spotted with a female at a hospital, she must mean something to him for him to either be at an appointment with her or be visiting someone with her. On the other hand, if the glass is half-full, he would suggest that she might be a family member or a close friend, or even an ex-girlfriend that was telling him she was getting married or something else innocent.

The suspense was killing her. She had no idea which way he would go. He definitely didn't look like he was swaying towards the half-full side. She decided it was time to just ask him what he thought.

"So what do you think I, I mean Justine should do?"

"I don't have a lot of advice for Justine, but I do have advice for you, Sis." Joelle knew that such a ruse wouldn't work on Jonah. Both he and Joshua Jr. knew how to read her and they often read her well.

"How long have you been in love with him?" *Where did that come from?* Joelle thought. *Why would Jonah go there?* she wondered.

"Why would you ask me that, Jonah?" As soon as she asked the question she looked away.

How could Jonah know something that she wasn't willing to admit out loud. This something definitely entered her mind, but she dismissed it because it was too ludicrous to even entertain such a thing. Afterall, she hadn't known X for a substantial amount of time. These feelings shouldn't be so strong from a glimpse outside of his bookstore, a business meeting where she was the epitome of professional, and a brief meeting in her hospital room. And yet, during all three encounters Joelle felt something for him that was incredibly and indescribably strong. She was drawn to him physically and mentally. Her emotions were all over the place.

Joelle was so caught up in her thoughts that she hardly heard Jonah's follow-up line of questions. What she could piece together was does X know how she feels about him, and if not, when will she let him know? The one thing that Joelle appreciated her brother was his candidness. He was never one to side-step and issue. He would be the first to tell someone male or female how he felt about him or her. So it was not a surprise he was in favor of Joelle putting everything, especially her heart, on the line by telling X how she felt. In the past, Joelle would not only listen to Jonah's advice when dealing with the opposite sex, she would actually take it. He may have had little success with his own relationships, but he knew how to school her in areas of men. Joelle didn't give him an answer, but pondered what he told her well after her had family left.

The family finally left after all three men successfully ate up all of her leftovers and her mom and Justine made sure she had everything she needed within reaching distance of her bed. Justine arrived just as the clan was packing up to leave. When Joelle mentioned that she needed to speak with Justine, she quickly ran behind the rest of the family and said she only wanted to see her face to make sure she was okay and that she planned on leaving soon after. Joelle knew that was a lie, but despite being mad at her for sharing her personal information with her family, she was glad Justine did as Joelle was truly unnerved by her hospital stay. She knew that Justine was aware of this and that's the reason she lied to the family. They made sure to place all of her medication along with a glass of water on one nightstand.

They placed snacks for her to nibble on on the other nightstand. She was not much of a snacker, but she figured she would indulge just for tonight to keep her mind off of what she would say when and if X called. She told herself that she didn't care if he did, but deep in her heart she was hoping he would. Joelle must have dozed off. She looked at the clock and it read 10:00 p.m. She was surprised no one had called her to check on her since five when they all left. She was only disappointed by one person in particular not calling. Just as she was about to reach for a pain pill, she felt a vibration underneath her. Somehow she managed to sleep on the phone. However, she didn't know why she hadn't heard it before. She checked it and saw that it was Justine.

"Hey, Justine."

"Girl, I was about to come over and use my emergency key to get into your house. I thought that maybe you fell out of bed or something. I called you twice." Joelle was still a little groggy, but she managed to become coherent enough to convince her friend that she was okay. After she hung up, she decided to check if she had missed any other calls. Her heart stopped when she saw that X had called.

He had called at 7:00 p.m., which was a respectful hour. That was very honorable considering some men have no problem with calling after 10:00 p.m. for what most likely is often a booty call. Now she wondered if she should call him back or wait for him to call her. Afterall, she was not used to being the aggressor. She wasn't exactly used to men falling all over her either, but she did get consecutive calls from men in the beginning of the courtship. After they found they were not getting the cookies, the calls seemed to die down. Joelle looked at the clock again. *I can't call him now*, she thought. It was after 10:00 p.m. But what the heck, both she and he were twenty-one plus. Just as she was calling his number she could see on her caller ID that he was calling her at the exact moment. Hesitantly, she clicked over. She didn't know quite what to say. She decided she would wait for him to say something first. After an awkward silence she heard X say hello and ask her if it was too late for him to be calling.

Joelle could hear the sincerity in his voice. He seemed genuinely concerned that he had woken her up.

"No, it's not too late for you to be calling. I'm actually glad you called. I've been thinking about you."

X couldn't believe what he heard. He couldn't believe that she said she was thinking about him. He damn sure was thinking about her all day. He was apprehensive about calling her. He had picked up the phone many times and dialed her number. He couldn't pull the trigger. Finally at 7:00 p.m., he made the call from his bookstore. He needed to talk to her more than he needed air to breathe, and he couldn't handle not knowing how she was doing. When he saw her in the hospital, his heart all but crumbled into pieces. His brother's interruption had prevented him from inquiring any further. He was so bothered, he was only half listening to his brother describing Xeria's weak explanation about how she ended up in the hospital. He and the rest of the family decided to give her some space and not pressure her. They knew she would eventually tell them what was going on.

In the meantime, they decided to keep a close eye and ear out for any calls by Deval. They didn't know how he was involved, but he definitely was indirectly responsible for her being at the house Xavier found her in. After Xeria was discharged and the family got her settled in in her condo, he left the family wanting to see Joelle. He wanted to get her opinion on how he should proceed with Xeria. Even though they had technically just met, there was a level of trust he had in her that he didn't quite understand. All he knew was that she would have the much-needed counsel he needed. He thought about going back to the hospital or even calling the hospital, but he didn't want to appear like a stalker. She did say it was okay to call, but he wanted to wait to give her time to rest if she was, in fact, released from the hospital.

And if her family was anything like his, they would stay with her to ensure that she was alright. He was at the bookstore when he made the call. He dared not go home after leaving Xeria given that his grand opening was only a week away. The phone system was up and running. All that was left was the security system and he had to wait for the massive shipment of books, bibles, music C's and DV's to come in. He, with the help of his family, would start putting things on the shelves next week. He wasn't sure how much help his family would be with Xeria being somewhat out of commission.

In fact, he was even considering asking Joelle to help him. But, in light of everything that was going on with her, he knew he couldn't ask her now. After tiding everything up, and wavering back and forth, he made the 7:00 p.m. call. She didn't answer. Maybe she was resting. He decided he would go home and call her later. He locked up the bookstore and headed home. On his way there, he stopped and grabbed a bite to eat. He to home at 7:45 p.m. After gulping down his food, he decided to lay down and take a quick nap. What was supposed to be a thirty-minute nap turned into a three-hour nap. He woke up after ten o'clock. He had had the most invigorating, sensuous dream about Joelle. It was so vivid. He could actually taste her lips and smell her hair in his dream. He woke up in a cold sweat and reached over to grab for her. When he didn't feel her, his eyes searched his room for her.

At that moment, he knew he had to call her. He second-guessed himself when he glanced at the clock again. It was 10:45 p.m. He decided to roll the dice and call her. After all he and she were over twenty-one. He needed to find out if she was okay whether she was still in the hospital or at home. However, if she was still in the hospital, he would keep it brief so as to avoid her getting reprimanded from one of the nurses for disturbing the others on the floor. However, if she was at home, he would speak with her until she said good night while still keeping in mind she was still recuperating.

"I've been thinking about you today as well. I called you at 7:00 p.m. and when you didn't answer, I told myself I would call you later. But I was exhausted after coming from getting ready for the grand opening, and I fell asleep."

Joelle didn't care if he had called her at 10:45 p.m. or 2:00 in the morning. It was nice hearing his sultry voice. He was definitely what the doctor ordered. She was so relieved to hear he was thinking of her as well. That suggested that maybe the mysterious woman was a relative or a close friend and not his significant other.

"The doctor gave me a clean bill of health. He told me to take it easy for a couple of days." Joelle surprised herself by sharing this personal information with him. In her spirit, she felt like he cared and would want to know this information about her condition.

"I have to see for myself, Joelle. Can I come by tomorrow just to make sure you are okay. I will leave soon after. Scout's honor."

Joelle couldn't help but chuckle at the thought of him being in a Scout uniform. She actually pictured him as a ten-year-old boy, wearing those khaki shorts and a greenish shirt. He probably went camping and earned all of his merit badges. Joelle's brothers had been in the troop at their church when growing up, so she knew all too well what was involved in Scouting. Joelle wished she had known him as a child. She was confident that if they had met a children, they would be married and have at least one child by now. She didn't know much about his family, except that he had a brother. She could tell he may have had at least one other sibling based on the interaction between the two men. She could surmise that that particular sibling may have been the person he came to see the day he wandered into her hospital room.

"Mr. Lawerence, I'm fine. There is no need for you to trouble yourself with coming over to see me."

Joelle contemplated having him come over, but she immediately remembered the woman she saw him with at the hospital. She still didn't know who she was. Even if she was family, she still wasn't certain. She wasn't sure if she should bring it up now or wait until a different occasion. Part of her wanted to hold off as long as possible. If he was involved, Joelle would gracefully back away from the situation. Joelle firmly believed that what God had for her was for her. As a result, if X belonged to someone else, he was not for her. Despite the connection, she was willing to walk away. Also, if she held off, then technically she shouldn't be held accountable. Afterall, isn't it his responsibility to let the woman know that he is involved. She can deduce that he's a Christian just like she is and undoubtedly he has read the bible. He knows what it says about lying and so forth. Her thoughts were interrupted when he again asked about coming to see her tomorrow. The moment of truth. What should she say? She said a quick silent prayer for guidance.

CHAPTER 20

X felt that he may have jumped the gun asking to come over and see her. He sensed that there was mutual attraction between them. All the signs were there from the business meeting, the phone conversation after the meeting, and their encounter at the hospital. Although, he could tell from their business meeting that she was definitely trying to keep it professional. She didn't want to provide him with anything personal at the meeting or over the phone, which was fine. He saw it as a challenge; a challenge that he was willing to undertake happily. After seeing her in the hospital, he knew then and there that he was going to do whatever it took to get inside her heart. She was definitely already in his.

Finally, Joelle gave him the answer he was hoping for. She said that she would see him tomorrow, but not at her house. She was feeling better and agreed to meet him at a place called Uncle Joe's. He was vaguely familiar with the place. He had heard that it had been taken over by a woman. He admired the new owner after reading an article about her in the local paper. From what he heard, she had transformed it from a sports bar into a high-end, upscale restaurant with the faint touch of down-home cooking. He was anxious to see her tomorrow. He wanted to see her, to touch her, to breathe her in. Above all, he just wanted to make sure she was okay. His phone rang. He immediately checked the caller ID hoping it was not Joelle canceling their date. He didn't recognize the number.

Fearing that it was something concerning his sister, he picked up. It was Xeria. He didn't know whose phone she was using. Before he would get into that, he decided to first play it cool and make her feel comfortable. It was extremely important that he tread lightly. When Xavian, Xavier, and their father dropped her off at home, she swore to them all that she would be okay by herself. Being the elder sibling, Xavian wanted to stay, but he had to get home to watch the twins while his wife went back to work to finish up paperwork on an important account. When their father suggested that she stay with him for the evening, she all but freaked out and again insisted that they leave. After calming her down, the men made a hasty retreat. They made sure she had food and painkillers on the nightstand. They gave her instructions to call no matter how late the hour if she needed anything, including a listening ear. X couldn't believe that two women he cared greatly about were released the same day from the hospital with injuries that were unbeknownst to him.

"What's going on, Xeria? How are you feeling?" X tried to stay calm and let Xeria ease into the conversation. He knew that she would eventually get out what she needed to get out.

"I'm doing well. I wanted to tell you what happened, but I need you to promise that you will not get angry. I need you to be a listener and not a judge."

After promising not to say anything, he listened to Xeria explain an addiction that he would have never guessed she had in a million years. First, Xeria explained that Deval introduced her to the world of underground gambling. What X couldn't understand was what made this type of gambling different from legal gambling in Atlantic City casinos, or even closer at the two new casinos built in the last two years in the tri-state area. Xeria stated that Deval ran a casino out of his basement along with two of his thug buddies. The customers were up-and-coming thugs/ gangster wannabes that enjoyed the risk associated with the underground gambling. They liked the thrill and the danger associated with it. There was a $500 cover charge just to get in the door.

"At first, X, I refused to participate in the activities. I told him that I had no interest in wasting my hard earned money on gambling. Deval kept pushing the issue; he even stated that he would waive the cover fee for me every time I played. Eventually, I decided to play a hand of poker. After winning a few hands, I was hooked. I was spending almost $200 a week there. By the end of the month, I was in the hole, and instead of encouraging me to stop, Deval stood by and watched as I started to spiral out of control. After all, this was business and money was money. When I found myself unable to pay my $10,000 marker, I got pressure from Deval's business partners. They approached me stating that they didn't care whose girl I was, they wanted their money. What surprised me X was that Deval didn't say a word. He just let them threaten me.

"At that point I knew that Deval was nothing more than a user. His name was so much like the "deceiver," that it's amazing that I never made this connection before. I thank God for you and the rest of my praying family. It was your prayers that opened my eyes to who Deval really was. With this discovery, I actually feared for my safety. I decided to go to Dad for a loan. I really hated getting him involved, but I had no other choice. I went to the church looking for Dad. Instead, I found Deacon Williams. I was in the sanctuary praying and crying when Deacon Jamison came in. He offered his shoulder. I was a little apprehensive at first, optics is crucial in a church. How would it look, the daughter of the minister crying on the shoulder of a married deacon? But I felt comfortable with Deacon Williams. He was like a father figure and at that moment, I felt like God answered my silent prayer by sending an angel for me to speak with.

"When I revealed to him my addiction, he surprised me by saying that he had a similar addiction. He started off with horse races. He kept a smile on his face every Sunday, while he was financially draining his account. He told me that when he finally hit rock bottom, he had no choice but to tell his wife. 'God is good,' he proclaimed. His wife not only forgave him, but she promised that she would stick by him and help him through his addiction. He said he would give me the money to cover the loan and he gave me a number to a Gamblers Anonymous support group. He even said he would be my sponsor. The only person that would have to know would be his wife as he vowed that he would not have any more secrets from her.

"I agreed and promised to pay him back and attend the support group. I was anxious and a little scared, but I went over to Deval's house to give him the money. His house is in one of the worst neighborhoods in Philadelphia. The police rarely go to that neighborhood because it is so bad. His house looked better than the other ones on the block, though. Two doors down from his house was a crack house, and on the corner was a house where they held illegal dog fights. X, I really hated going to his neighborhood. The night he introduced me to gambling was the first time he brought me to his house. Usually, we hung out at my place or we went out to a movie or restaurant. Gambling had me doing things and going places that were not safe. I believed that the sooner I gave Deval the money, the sooner he would be out of my life. I went on a night before the gambling started in the basement. He tried to kiss me on the cheek, but I moved away and extended the money for him to take. He yelled and cursed at me.

"At that moment, I didn't know who this man was standing in front of me. He started out so charming and sweet, but now he was pure evil. He stated that he would be connected to me throughout all eternity. I thought he was only bluffing. After all, the bible says, *No weapon formed against me shall prosper.* I knew that God would get me through this. So, again I tried to hand him the money, but he refused to take it. I placed it on the coffee table and started to get up and leave. As I turned around, he grabbed my arm. I broke free, and he slapped me hard in the face and kicked me in my abdomen."

X, at this point, felt the heat rushing to his face.

"I stumbled over and fell on his couch."

He wanted to get to Deval and hurt him bad, like he hurt his sister. Xeria could tell that he was about to blow.

"I need you to calm down, X, or I will hang up and not tell you the rest of the story."

X had to fight past the anger, because he needed to know the full story before he stepped in and took care of Deval. X assured her that he was fine and asked her to finish the story. X could tell that she was rushing through the rest of the story before she lost her nerve.

"He told me that he loved me and would not let me go. He walked over to the couch and sat down calmly while watching me struggle to my feet. I was really scared."

X could hear faint sniffles in her voice.

"When he didn't move to prevent me from leaving, I made my way to the front door holding my stomach. I tried to make it to my car, but I couldn't. Just when I thought I was about to pass out, someone was right beside me trying to hold me up. I didn't know where the person was leading me, I was too weak to protest. I was placed on a bed and soon sleep overtook me."

X couldn't believe what he was hearing. It was like a scene from a gangster movie he had seen. He was grateful that the woman at the crack house took care of his sister in her time of need. God can use anyone. For a brief moment, X thought about Deacon Brown. He felt a sense of relief to hear that she was not having an affair with someone in her father's church. He never really believed that she would do such a thing, but Xeria's unpredictable behavior suggested that she was capable of anything, just like most Christians. The thing about being a Christian is that people think that once you accept Jesus Christ as your personal savior, life is easy and a bowl of cherries.

When actuality, it's the opposite. As soon as you accept Jesus, that is when the devil really gets on your trail. The devil knows that once you are in God's hands, there is nothing he can do to pluck you out. But since he is the enemy and his job is to kill and destroy, he may throw all hell at you to keep you from seeing that. He tries to destroy reputations and relationships. If X hadn't known his sister better than she knew herself, he would have been tempted to believe something that would ruin her reputation, like an affair with a married man. Anger resurfaced again and X wanted to go over to Deval's place and beat the hell out of him. Xeria could read his mind. She made him promise not to do anything to

Deval. She reminded him the Lord's point of view about vengeance. Before X could protest, Xeria's other line rang. She placed him on hold to answer another call.

"X, it's my job. I have to take this call. I promise I'll call you back when I finish." Xeria told him she loved him and hung up the phone.

X contemplated calling their father and sharing the conversation, but he thought better. He didn't want to break Xeria's confidence just yet, but he would eventually share with his father because he knew that Xeria needed his prayer and covering. He decided to watch television and focus on what he would say during his date tomorrow with Joelle. Again he realized he was faced with yet another mystery surrounding a woman he cared greatly about. He hadn't found out the reason behind Joelle's hospital visit. Sure, she said she was recovering nicely, but he didn't know from what. He prayed that her situation was less dramatic than his sister's or he would find himself in another battle.

CHAPTER 21

Joelle woke up the next morning excited. She tried to get a handle on her emotions. She was excited about seeing X, but she still had unanswered questions about the mystery woman. Today would be the day she would find out who she was. She refused to leave the meeting today without having a clear understanding of their relationship. If he was involved, she would sever ties except for those associated with his phone system. She decided to look for something to wear before jumping in the shower.

They were scheduled to meet up around twelve noon. This was a perfect time for a date. It gave both parties the opportunity to schedule a second activity after they parted ways if needs be. Her father already scheduled her off for the day and the rest of the week, so she did not have to return to work. She already knew that she would hang out at Uncle Joe's after he left to fill Justine in on what occurred. Even if she wanted to leave, she knew that her friend wouldn't allow it until she spilled the beans. Justine was just as curious and invested in finding out who the mystery woman was as Joelle. She checked the time. She had three hours to get ready and get to Uncle Joe's. She found the perfect outfit for her lunch date. It was not too sexy, but it was tastefully simple. She was about to find the right pumps to accentuate the outfit when she heard her cell phone ringing from her bedroom. She picked up the phone, expecting to hear her mother, her father, one of or her brothers, or Justine checking up on her this morning.

"Yes, Mother, Father, Brothers, or Justine, I am fine. I took my morning meds, and I am about to jump in the shower." Joelle listened for an answer before checking the phone. It was X. Before she could say something, he spoke.

"Well, I was waiting for you to say my name. I was hoping that after you called off the names of your family and friends you would call off the name of someone else that cared about you."

"And who would that be, Mr. Lawerence, pray tell? Who cares about me other than my family?"

X smirked. Joelle was toying with him, but he was enjoying it. She had to know that he felt something for her. She had to know that she had won a place in his heart. However, if she didn't he would spend this afternoon showing her just how much she meant to him.

"Why, Ms. Jamison, I think you know the answer to that question."

Joelle felt her cheeks warming. She read romance novels about women blushing, but she never thought it applied to women of color. That was until she looked at herself in the mirror as she grabbed her toothpaste from the medicine cabinet. When she closed the door, she saw a touch of red in her cheeks. She would never have believed it if she hadn't been looking at herself in the mirror. She listened to X while trying to quietly brush her teeth. Her responses were limited to more sounds than words. Once she was done, she went straight into her walk-in closet to get dressed. She was confident the outfit would wow him.

"Well, Mr. Lawerence I can't assume anything when it comes to you and our relationship. I am a do-tell type of person. Those in my circle do tell me how they feel, so there is no need for assumptions where they are concerned."

X was tempted to tell her that he not only cared for her, but was willing to give up his very life for her. He didn't want to come off too strong, so he settled for telling her that he cared about people that he does business with. He could sense a little disappointment in her voice, but what was he supposed to tell her? Would she be accepting of the strong feelings he felt for her, or would she be scared off? She hung up the phone kind of hastily. He knew that he would have to smooth things over when he met her. He didn't want her to be angry with him, but before he would give her any more of his heart, he had to know how she felt about him, even if it meant temporarily hurting her.

Joelle got off the phone and put the finishing touches to her look. She was determined to be on time. Since her demotion, she had gotten to work on time 100% of the time. She hoped her father was being made aware of this by her brother and would soon recognize that she deserved her old position back. She put on her new pair of skinny jeans and a V-neck top that showed just a touch of cleavage. Her mother always taught her to keep it classy. She decided to put on a tiny bit of makeup and some lip gloss just to give her lips a shine. She glanced at the clock sure that it was probably only 11:00 a.m. She had an hour to get to Uncle Joe's. She checked herself out in the mirror and then glanced at the clock.

"You've got to be kidding me!" She wiped her eyes in disbelief. She couldn't believe that the clock said 11:45 a.m. instead of 11:00 a.m. Where did the time go? She couldn't believe that it was this late. She grabbed her jacket and headed out the door in a hurry. It typically took her twenty minutes to get to Uncle Joe's without traffic. Putting her keys in the ignition, she said a quick prayer that she would make every light and not be behind any Sunday morning drivers on a Tuesday morning.

X looked at his watch. It was now 12:30. Somewhere in the pit of his stomach, he felt that Joelle might have changed her mind about their innocent rendezvous today. He was hoping that she didn't, but he sensed a little apprehension in her voice the last time they spoke. He offered up a prayer that she was first and foremost all right, then that she was on her way. When he had gotten there earlier, he told the hostess that he was meeting someone and that he would be waiting at the bar. He was a little uncomfortable at the bar because he didn't drink, so at 12:15 p.m. he asked to be seated. The hostess gave him a strange look, but then escorted him to his table. At 12:20 p.m. he called Joelle on her cell and left a message asking if he was at the correct restaurant. He called again at 12:25 sharing his concern for her physical well-being. Now at 12:30, as he looked up from his watch, he didn't know what to do. He signaled for the waitress. As she was walking over to him, another beautiful woman stopped her. They had a brief conversation and the waitress turned and walked the other way. The woman proceeded to walk over to his table.

"Hello Mr. Lawerence."

X surmised that she must have gotten his name from the hostess. X recognized her as the new owner of Uncle Joe's, but he didn't remember her name. He couldn't remember it from the article; all he remembered was the extremely flattering picture of her. What he didn't know was why she was at his table with an intense look on her face.

"So, you know my name; may I ask yours?"

Justine liked this new man in Joelle's life. He seemed confident and charming at the same time.

"Mr. Lawerence, my name is Justine. It is a pleasure to meet you." X extended his hand towards her to grasp it in a handshake. Her grip was strong. "I'm also Joelle's best friend."

Now X had an inkling about why she was here. However, he was hoping she wasn't here to tell him that Joelle would be canceling their date. Or worse, she had been in some terrible accident due to rushing to her date with him. He knew she had a problem with lateness, but it wasn't worth dying over. He knew that he would wait for her until eternity if necessary. Before Justine could open her mouth to say another word, he caught a glimpse of Joelle coming through the door. She was definitely flustered. She spoke to the hostess who then pointed her in X's direction. Justine politely excused herself and made a beeline to her friend. They gave each other a quick embrace and had a short conversation before Joelle made her way over to X.

X gave her a quick up-down perusal. He knew that she would feel uncomfortable if he gawked at her for too long, even though that's exactly what he wanted to do. He could look at her all day and every day. She looked beautiful from head to toe. Casual for the establishment they were in, however there was a touch of sexy as well. She showed just the right amount of cleavage to temp any suitor into trying to get a better peek at what lay beneath that delicate fabric. Her jeans fit her hips nicely and the wedge sandals really accentuated her look and gave her just the right amount of height for his liking. The other times he had seen her, except in the hospital, she looked great. Today however, she had a glow.

As she got closer, X could catch a whiff of her scent. It was the same scent she had worn to their first encounter at his bookstore. It was a light citrus smell that may have been subtle to anyone else, but not to him. For him it was a trigger and aroused all parts of his anatomy. Her hair was done differently since he had seen her last. She had loose soft curls that framed her face cascading down one side of her face. The strands on the other side were tucked securely behind her ear. X could tell that she was unaware of how strikingly beautiful she was. If she had known, she wouldn't have had her hair covering her beauty. X would make it a point to tell her just how beautiful she was on a daily basis, so she not only knew it but felt it in the core of her being.

X stood and extended his hand out to her to help her take a seat. They were seated in a booth in the rear of the restaurant. Usually X preferred being closer to the exit in the event of an emergency, but today he made an exception when he saw how cozy the rear of the restaurant was. Even in the early afternoon, the soft décor was meant for couples that craved intimacy. The colors, tapestries, and photos made it a hybrid between sports bar and fine dining establishment. At the front was a picture of the previous owner Uncle Joe. X hoped that the same positive energy he found in this place could be generated in his establishment when his store was up and running. Before the opening, he would have his family and friends over for a blessing ceremony. Because everything belongs to God, X wanted to dedicate a ceremony giving honor to God for blessing him with such a powerful and prayerfully profitable way of ministering to God's people.

Joelle sat across from X mesmerized by how fine he was. She was grateful he didn't leave. When she started out to Uncle Joe's, she couldn't believe how much traffic was out this morning. When she turned off South Broad street she found herself in a traffic nightmare. Something told her to take the side streets, but she hadn't anticipated this many cars on the road on a Tuesday. She knew that there would be a few people out on their lunch break, but she underestimated how many Philadelphians preferred to drive to lunch instead of walking, especially with gas being so expensive. She took X's hand but still managed to sit down in a huff. She hoped he couldn't see how frazzled she was. Her gaze met his. There was an aura of masculinity and strength that was coming across the table that sent electric shocks through her. She didn't know what to say. She was drowning in his dark eyes and needed a life jacket just to keep her afloat. Reluctantly, she broke her gaze with X and started thinking about the brief conversation she had with Justine when she arrived.

"Are you okay, Joelle?" Justine had asked. Joelle listened as Justine frantically explained how worried X looked because of her tardiness.

"When you called to tell me to relay the message to X that you were going to be late, I thought the worst. And then when the call was dropped, I went bananas."

As Justine was talking, Joelle watched as X's eyebrow elevated. Joelle knew she had to thank and reassure her friend fast that she was alright so she could get to her man. Wow, her man. Joelle liked the sound of that. Now that she was across from him, she couldn't think of anything to say. She knew she would have to explain her lateness. She started with talking about what she called a traffic gridlock. Then she started talking so fast that he didn't know what she was saying. He held up his one finger to his lips to signify that she didn't have to explain any further.

He enjoyed watching her beautiful, sumptuous lips move a mile a minute, but he didn't want her nerves to get the best of her and cause her any unnecessary stress. What he would tell her later was that time meant nothing to him. He would have waited until the end of time for her. In the back of his mind, he thought she might be late, but he never thought that she would not show at all. He knew that she was meant for him. She was his Eve, Sarah, Ruth. X was not to fond of all those Christian clichés, especially since most were not biblically sound, but he agreed with the one that said "Let go and let God." He had been searching for his rib since his last relationship failed. When he let God take the lead, he sent Joelle into his life. He just hoped she would hearken to God's plan for them and open her heart up to him and eventually the two would become one.

"Just breathe, Joelle. I was willing to wait as long as I had to for you."

Joelle couldn't believe what she just heard. She had never heard anyone say they were willing to wait forever for her. During one date, when she arrived ten minutes late, the guy candidly told her how precious his time was and how she needed to be mindful of that for the next date. Needless to say, there was no next date. Where others may have viewed her actions as being self-centered, she thought that men should wait for her because she was spending the extra time to get ready to make herself pretty for them. She thought they should give her a little slack. Now if she was more than an hour late, she understood the irritation. That's why she was grateful X didn't leave. Even though she had no idea the traffic would be that bad, she still would have understood if he left. Spending a day in the hospital showed her how time should not be taken for granted or taken advantage of.

As livid as she was by the demotion due to her lateness, she discovered it had been a blessing in disguise. Since her demotion she had been on time every day except the original appointment she had with X that she had to maneuver to another time. The bible speaks about the importance of discipline. She was grateful that her father chose to step in before her small tardiness problem turned into a bigger problem that affected her character, integrity, and reputation as an efficient businesswoman.

"What would you like to eat?"

Joelle needed something to cool her down and off. She caught a glimpse of X's lips as such a simple question rolled off his kissable lips. They were full and she knew that once he covered hers with them, she wouldn't want him to ever stop.

"Umm, I better check the menu," Joelle said sheepishly.

X knew that this was a stall tactic. This, after all, was her best friend's restaurant. Not only did she know what was on the menu, she had probably tasted everything on the menu. But X was okay with waiting on her because it meant he would be spending time with her. He still didn't know the cause of her hospitalization, but he didn't want to bring the subject up just yet. He didn't want to weigh down their first date with such a serious topic. He knew he had time to talk about serious stuff later. For right now, he just wanted to look at her and hopefully at the end of the date get the first much anticipated kiss. They placed their order with the waitress and handed her back the menus. After ten minutes of conversation, he felt his phone buzzing in his pocket. He started not to check it, but he didn't have that luxury with everything going on with Xeria.

When Joelle insisted that he take the call, he excused himself.

Being a female, she of course was curious about who was calling him, especially since they were technically on a date.

"I'm sorry Joelle. An emergency has come up. I have to leave. I will call you as soon as I can to reschedule our next date."

X leaned in and kissed her tenderly on her cheek. This was not the first kiss he wanted, but it would have to do. With that, he was gone. Joelle just sat there not knowing what to think or what to do. She considered that maybe her lateness was the real reason he had to leave. She was starting to understand what her father was trying to teach her. She just hoped it was not too late to turn this train around and get it back on track.

CHAPTER 22

X was extremely upset by his expedited departure. He really didn't want to have to leave Joelle, but he received a call from Xeria. Something was wrong. She was rambling on about being at their father's cabin in the Poconos. She needed to get away for a while to sort things out. She stated that Deval had been calling her nonstop since she got out of the hospital. She paid him the $10,000.00 so she wanted no more parts of him. He had left many messages apologizing for what he did and asking her to forgive him. She kept ignoring his calls. She stated that before she left, she stopped and paid Deacon Williams the $10,000.00 and headed out for a relaxing weekend in the Poconos. The only person she told was her friend Reni.

Apparently, Reni thought that they were still together and she told Deval where she was. It takes an hour and a half to get to the cabin. Xeria thinks that he is on his way up there. She had taken him there once before, so he knows exactly where the cabin is located. X was on his way to pick up his father and brother. He would fill them in on everything that was going on when they got in the car. X wished he would have told his father what was going on with Xeria sooner, like he intended, but that ship had sailed. He just prayed his father wouldn't be too upset with his decision to honor Xeria's privacy a little while until he figured out what to do.

"What's going on son?" His dad and brother where not in the car for one minute before his father wanted in on what was going on. He was surprised Xavian was at their dad's place. Xavian said that when he told them there was an emergency with Xeria, Xavian decided to go to their dad's house to save time. X was anxious about what his father was going to say. He watched his father's reaction through the mirror and glanced sideways at this brother's profile to gauge his reaction to the information he was sharing about their sister. He saw Xavian's hands clenched into a tight fist. When X found out, he was ready to beat the living crap out of Deval. Being the eldest brother, he knew Xavian was ready to kill Deval.

"How could you keep this information from us?" Xavian was practically screaming at his brother. X thought that he was going to punch something. He was praying his brother wasn't going to punch him while he was behind the wheel. Just as he was about to respond, his father interrupted them and asked them to do something that was typical of a preacher. He asked them to stop talking and start praying. Xavian immediately stopped speaking and bowed his head as their father offered up a prayer.

"Father God, I come to you on behalf of my beloved child. I am asking that you let no harm come to her while we rush to get her out of harm's way. When they placed this precious gift we named Xeria into my arms, I vowed to protect her. I am asking that you help me to honor that vow by being in the mist with her and building a hedge around her. She is the apple of your eye and a beautiful woman inside and out. Please turn what the enemy has meant for harm into good, I pray. Amen.

Both X and Xavian repeated Amen. At that moment, there was a peace that was shifting the atmosphere from chaos and uncertainty to calm and assurance that all would be well with Xeria. When they pulled up to the cabin, they saw Xeria's car and a black GMC truck. Before X could bring the car to a complete stop, Xavian was out of the car. He was glad his father prayed, but he knew when it came to Xeria, his wife, and twin sons, Xavian could be a minister with a bear of a punch. He prayed if Deval was here, he would at least be able to walk out under his own accord. But he couldn't make any promises. Xavian kicked open the door. X and their father were two steps behind him. X looked around and was in total shock. The cabin was in shambles. There had definitely been a battle in the room. X called out for Xeria. Nothing. He ran to one of the bedrooms, while Xavian checked the basement. It was locked. Xavian called him and his father over.

Xeria! Xeria!. It's Xavian, X, and Dad. Are you down there?" X could hear the anxiety in Xavian's voice. He, too, was anxious and scared. He didn't know what they would find. The door was unlocked and out stepped a wobbly, badly bruised Xeria. She fell to the floor as their father caught her. Out of the corner of their eye, they saw a figure run for the door. It was Deval. Before he knew it, X was all over Deval with Xavian right beside him. He was administering blows to Deval's face and abdomen at what seemed like the speed of light. Xavian had to pull him off. X thought he did so to save Deval life, but instead it was to get in a few good licks himself.

"Enough, boys!" their father yelled. Call the police and let them deal with him. We have your sister to worry about." Instantly both gentlemen hearkened to their father's voice.

When the police arrived, they took a report. Because Deval was so badly beaten, both Xavian and X were to be taken to the local jail. Mr. Lawerence was allowed to take Xeria to the hospital while they were taking a report of the events that occurred there that night.

"Wait!" Deval stated, the rasp in his voice making both X and Xavian feel a little bad for the beatdown, although well deserved. The two officers placed X and Xavian in cuffs and placed them on the couch. Both officers seemed to not fully understand what was about to happen, but there was a shift in the atmosphere that was flipping the script.

"Xeria mentioned that one of you was a preacher. After I saw what I did to Xeria, I immediately felt sick to my stomach. I retreated to the bathroom due to shame. I deserve what I got. If someone would have hurt my sister like I hurt yours, they wouldn't even be breathing once I got through. He knew neither X or Xavian knew where he was going with this monologue, but he hoped they would continue listening patiently.

"Would you mind praying for me and asking God to forgive me for my actions?"

X and Xavian looked at each other and thanked God for working in mysterious ways.

"Have you accepted Jesus as your personal savior?" asked Xavian.

"No," Deval stated and X thought he saw a tear slide down Deval's face.

When asked, the officers acquiesced by taking off the two gentlemen's handcuffs and allowed them to place their hands on Deval to pray for him. Their father's prayer had come to fruition. What the enemy meant for evil, God used it for good. After the prayer, X and Xavian were placed back in cuffs and taken to the police station. They were released in the morning. They immediately took a cab back to the cabin to pick up their car and headed to the hospital to check on Xeria.

X and Xavian reached the hospital in no time and were quickly told what room Xeria was in. When they got to her hospital room, they greeted their father with a warm hug outside in the hallway. "How's she doing, Dad?"

"She'll be okay, but the damage Deval did was extensive and with this being the second round of damage to her abdomen area, she will need to be hospitalized for at least a month. After their father gave them more details, Xavian excused himself to make a quick call to his wife to update her on what was happening. X walked over to Xeria and place a kiss on her cheek. He offered a prayer of thanks for her well-being and took a seat next to her at his father's instance. X fell asleep.

When he opened his eyes, he heard his sister's voice. She was talking to Xavian and their father. She looked over at X and started to cry.

"Hey, what are the tears for? You're okay now," X stated tenderly to his baby sister. At this moment, she looked so innocent and angelic. As if in a time machine, he was taken back to when she was a little girl running behind him and Xavian with pigtails flying haphazardly.

"I know, thanks to all of you." Xeria smiled.

X placed a kiss on her cheek and they all joined hands for another prayer of thanks. Heads bowed and hearts open, they were definitely a family that prayed together and would, with prayer, stay together.

Before X let go of his family's hands, he said a silent prayer that he would be able to make things right with Joelle. After almost losing Xeria, he knew that life was too short. He wanted Joelle to share his life more than any other thing in the world.

Chapter 23

Joelle was disappointed that X had to leave their date prematurely. She understood that there was a "family emergency" or so he said, but that didn't negate the fact that she was looking forward to spending the afternoon with him enjoying delicious food and intriguing conversation. After placing their order, he soon went into sharing details about himself, his family, and what gave him the idea of starting his own business, particularly a Christian bookstore.

Had she known that their date would be cut short, she would have started the conversation with an inquiry about the mysterious woman that he was communicating with at the hospital. The one bonus was that before he left, he inquired about a second date and placed the most endearing kiss on her cheek. She loved the softness of his lips against her skin. Joelle was already giddy about their next date. Before she knew it, a smile was plastered all over her face. A smile that Justine did not miss when she walked over to her table.

"What's got you all giddy? I just saw your man leave after being here for only ten minutes." Justine smirked.

"If you must know, I am smiling because I'm anticipating the next date."

"Okay, but did you get a chance to ask him about the mysterious woman?"

Joelle knew that Justine would be a buzzkill, so to speak. *Leave it to her to bust my euphoric bubble.* Justine has always been an inquisitive and no-nonsense person. She did not believe in beating around the bush when it came to men.

"We didn't get a chance to address it. He told me a lot about himself, though."

Joelle had already told Justine about X's one sibling. She learned today that he did in fact have another sibling. A sister, which she also told Justine about. She also shared the fact that his mother had died giving birth to said little sister. For some men, losing a parent can make him/her deficient in some areas. Joelle wondered if it was the same for X. So far he seemed "normal," but only time would tell. It's a good thing God knows the heart. She knew that if he had a relationship with the Lord, she would be okay in his hands if he was a single man of God. There are several men in the church who proclaim they love the Lord, but act in a ways that are completely opposite of God's will. Joelle could tell this was not the case with X. Not only was he grounded in the Lord, his whole family was.

"So what do you think of him?" Justine asked, breaking Joelle's concentration.

Joelle knew this would be her second question. Unfortunately she did not quite know how to answer it. Joelle knew that she was intrigued by this man and that she wanted to get to know him better. Even when she tried to find something wrong with him, she couldn't; well, outside of who the mysterious woman was. If anything, he would be guilty of infidelity if he was in a relationship with the woman she saw him with at the hospital.

"I like him, Justine. There is something masculine and mature about him that gets my juices flowing. I feel like there is an indescribable connection between the two of us that God has given his blessing on. Call me crazy, especially since we really only just met." Joelle smiled again.

Joelle didn't want to share too much because she knew Justine was a hopeless romantic. She wanted to find love and romance just as much as Joelle did. When Joelle prayed for her Boaz, she was on her knees praying for her friend as well. Joelle knew that the only man that could handle Justine, was someone that was strong and caring at the same time. Just as Joelle was about to share more about her thoughts and feelings about Mr. X, one of Justine's employees needed to steal her away. Joelle was glad for the reprieve. She took the opportunity to wave at her friend and signaled that she would call her later.

When she got home, she almost stepped on Jinx. He was waiting for her at the door purring and then circling her legs for a little TLC. On her drive home, she was still on cloud nine just thinking about the next time she would see X. They still had to work out the details of the where and when. It dawned on her that he didn't mention that he would call her this evening. That worried her a little bit, but all she could do was be hopeful. She wasn't bold enough to call him. No matter how she felt about him, in her eyes this just wasn't done. Her spirit told her that he would call, so she didn't worry about it.

She glanced at the clock and it read 7:00 p.m. She decided to make good use of her time by tidying up her apartment. Since being released from the hospital, her apartment didn't look that bad, but she did need to do laundry. Even though her father told her to take the week off, she would return to work tomorrow anyway. She missed conversing with her coworkers. Since her demotion, she learned the meaning of teamwork. In her former roles, she was used to delegating responsibilities to the people that worked with her. She respected them and what they did for the company. However, in her new role she was given more insight into the people she worked with. She saw that they were the backbone that made the company one of the top enterprises in the city.

She could tell that the individuals that worked at Jamison Telecommunications were first class. The Jamison family was fortunate to have them as not only employees, but friends. While she was ill, many of them inquired about her health and wished her well on her recovery. God was truly in the blessing business. Not only had he blessed her with a wonderful family, but she had wonderful friends and colleagues. Not many people were as fortunate as Joelle. She knew that she would be promoted back to her previous status, but she was a little apprehensive. She wondered if she would go back to her old ways, or if she would continue growing into the mature, responsible, dependable person that God was growing her to be.

Deep down she knew it would be hard not reverting back to her old habits, but Proverbs 3:13 says, "Blessed is the one who finds wisdom and the one who gets understanding." For the second time, she was grateful that God gave her father the wisdom to discipline her before her tardiness problem became the downfall of her professional career. Joelle looked up at the clock again. The hours had passed and still no call from Xavier. She checked her phone to make sure it wasn't on mute. It was fine. She hoped everything was okay with him. The phone call he received at the restaurant did seem to be intense. She could hear what she thought was a woman's voice on the other end, even though he was trying to be discreet.

She watched his face go from calm and cheerful to intense and infuriated. He did not lose his composure, though. He simply ended the call and explained that he had an emergency, and then he was gone. Joelle wondered if he was talking to the mystery woman from the hospital. Was she the reason for his abrupt change of mood? The one thing she could tell was that whatever their relationship was, she meant a great deal to him. Joelle sat down trying to recount everything about the phone call. She needed something, anything to help give her clarity on what type of relationship it was.

Just as she started to dissect and scrutinize it, she decided against it. Proverbs 19:21 says, "Many are the plans in the mind of man, but it is the purpose of the Lord that will stand." Joelle knew that she didn't have control over anything except herself and her feelings. Glancing at the clock, she knew she wouldn't be hearing from X tonight. He was too much of a gentleman to call at this late hour. Although a bit sad, she was still at peace and knew everything would be okay.

She decided to read the rest of Proverbs and afterwards she turned in. That night she got the best sleep ever.

It had been a week since Joelle had spoken to X. She got back in the routine of work and was promoted back to her former position. When her father told her that she would be leaving the sales position, she actually cried. Her coworkers threw her a farewell celebration and told her not to forget the "little people." She told them that she was just a phone call and a few floors away. Jonah helped her move her things back into her old office. Her mother was there as well with a bottle of non-alcoholic champagne and a congratulations hug. Joelle was reminded of the book of Job where God had given everything back to Job that he lost and more. Joelle had received a pay increase and the reward of handling all of the top VIP clients in the telephone division.

Joelle was grateful to God for the many blessings and yet she was short one—Xavier. Despite not hearing from him, she prayed for him every day on bended knee. She prayed that God was covering him and keeping him strong wherever he was. Justine had been upbeat and positive as well. She told her that they were made for each other and that God was still in the blessing business. Joelle was shocked by Justine's revelation. At that moment she knew the meaning of the saying "Let go and let God."

One night as she was about to leave, she received a call from the troubleshooting department. It was in reference to the phone system set up in Xavier's bookstore. She glanced at her calendar. His store's grand opening was the next day. She went back and forth about attending it. It was expected for her to show and congratulate him not only as a client of Jamison Telecommunications, but as a friend despite being MIA for about a week. According to the troubleshooting department, there was a signal problem on X's end. Someone would have to be sent out to the site to check the system because it was very extensive. Joelle decided she would go. Her father had insisted that all of his children learn any maintenance aspect that went along with their particular department. Because Joelle knew she would work in the telephone division, she took classes on how to fix and repair phone consoles while studying business in college. She checked the clock. It read five o'clock. Although she hated the idea of five o'clock traffic, she wanted to make sure everything was perfect for X's grand opening in the morning. She had gotten in the habit of making her parents and siblings aware of her whereabouts after her hospitalization.

If she didn't call them, they would certainly track her down if they couldn't get ahold of her. She dialed her two brother's extension and neither one answered. She tried her dad's extension with no luck either. Her last attempts were to her mother and Justine. Both calls went to voicemail. This was strange. She couldn't reach anyone in her family. This was super strange. Well, they couldn't get mad at her for not being available when they finally returned her phone call. She gathered her briefcase and loaded it with tools she may need to fix the problem; including her bible. If all else failed, she would find scripture to speak to the problem. She closed down her computer and was off.

As she was driving, she hadn't thought about what she would say to X if he was there. The trouble-shooting department told her that one of X's employees would be there to let her into the facility. Part of her hoped he would be there since she was eager to see him, but she didn't know what she would say to him. What if things between him and the mystery woman had progressed and he wanted to keep is strictly professional with her. At that moment, Joelle felt like she was about to have an anxiety attack. She decided to pull over to avoid causing an accident. To help her calm down, she decided to call Justine.

"Dang! Am I the only one that stays at work past 5:00 p.m.?" Joelle hit the End button and took a few deep breaths. She started to sing a hymn which calmed her down. Her favorite hymn was "It is Well with My Soul." After a few rounds of this, she restarted her car and eased back into traffic. Instantly, she felt a peace that passes all understanding. Whether X was there or not, involved with someone or not, Joelle knew that she would be all right. In Ezekiel it talks about God knowing the purpose he has created for our lives. Joelle pulled up to the bookstore. She saw one parked car in the lot. It was not X's so she could only conclude it was his employee's. Her heart sank, but she had work to do. She opened the car door and headed to the front door of the bookstore and knocked three times.

A woman answered the door. She explained that she was the employee that made the call to her troubleshooting department. Joelle looked around the store. It was truly beautiful inside. The décor was warming and inviting. She especially liked the corner designated for children. While still surveying the store, she could picture herself curled up in one of the big comfortable chairs strategically placed around the room reading one of the numerous spiritual books placed on the shelves. She hoped one day she would bring her own children there to share the word of God. X had truly done an outstanding job creating a sanctuary that would not only bless his patrons, but honor the God that we serve. Joelle was shown where the master system was located. She took out her tool box and said a quick prayer that she would not only diagnose the problem, but also find the most effective way to remedy the problem.

After ten minutes with no success, she started to worry. She wanted to get in and out because despite what she said about wanting to see X, she was now apprehensive. What if he walked in with the mysterious woman? Her heart couldn't take it. Before panic set in, she reached for her bible. Recently, she had been reading and depending more and more on God's word. A little unsteady, it slipped from her wobbling hands and it fell open. As she was stooping down to retrieve it, she felt the presence of someone behind he. She turned her head slowly and behind her was Xavier. He knelt down beside her and placed his hands over hers and the bible. Over his shoulder she saw the mystery woman standing next to his brother Xavian with his arms wrapped securely around her waist. Next to both of them was a man that she immediately identified as Xavier's father. What in the world was going on? Next to Xavier's family was her parents, two brothers, and Justine. She took her gaze off them and looked into Xavier's eyes.

"What's going on here?" Joelle asked nervously and with a whisper.

Xavier gently grabbed her hands and helped her to her feet. He bent back down and picked up the bible and placed it on the counter.

"Joelle, I know we haven't spoken in a week, but I have thought about you every moment since our date."

Joelle tried to remain calm, but she was a bit confused. Last she checked, phones were still operational. Why couldn't he have picked up the phone and called her if he was thinking about her? Before she could ask the question, Xavier silenced her with a light kiss. Joelle wondered what their first kiss would be like. She was not prepared for what she received. How can a man taste sweet and sensual at the same time?

"I knew from the moment I met you in my store that we had a special connection. I knew that God placed you in my life for a reason."

Joelle listened intently, still not sure why her family was present.

"The past week has been hell. Literally with issues concerning my sister, the opening of the store, and not being able to talk to you, I thought I was going to lose my mind. But it did make me realize that I needed someone in my life to be my helpmate, my Eve, Sara, Ruth. Joelle, I want that person to be you. I truly love, no I am truly in love with you."

Before Joelle could answer, he picked up the Bible from the counter. When he picked it up, he kept it open not knowing what it was turned to. Xaviar let out a chuckle.

"You can't tell him that this is not ordained. Listen to what passage the bible landed on.

"He who finds a wife finds a good thing and obtains favor from God." Proverbs 18:22.

Joelle saw this as confirmation as well. It then dawned on her that her attacks were not from anxiety; it was the love she had for him. The thought of not being with him caused her body anxiety. Before she knew it in one motion, Xaviar was down on one knee.

"Joelle Elizabeth Jamison, I love you. Will you marry me?"

Joelle started to cry. She thought she was having one of her attacks, but after looking into his eyes, she acknowledged she was in love.

"Yes. Yes. I love you too. Thank you, Lord." Joelle looked up to heaven to give thanks while Xaviar placed the ring on her finger. He swept her off her feet and placed a kiss on her lips.

"Wow, you taste sweet and sensual at the same time," Xavier whispered in Joelle's ear. The room exploded with applause and shouts of *Hallelujah*. The family gathered around the happy couple.

CHAPTER 24

It was a beautiful day for a wedding. Joelle couldn't believe this day had finally come. She thought three months was a long time to wait to marry the man she had fallen madly in love with, but the days went by so fast. With the wedding planning in super speed, she barely could catch her breath. She was thankful that her over-the-top, mom was more than willing to put her two cents in. Of course, being the first Jamison to have a full-scale wedding, money was no object. She also had a lot of help from an unexpected source; one of the mother's from X's father's church—Ms. Watson. She was glad X had her.

Apparently, she had known the family for years since X's mother passed away. It couldn't be easy for X planning his wedding without his mom. Even though his mom had gone on to glory many years past, Joelle could feel the pain of not having his mom with him on this day. Ms. Watson would be sitting at the family table. Joelle, Xeria, and Julia could all see that Ms. Watson had it bad for X's father. It was amazing that all of the men were oblivious to this. When Joelle tried to point it out to X, he insisted they were just good friends. Joelle didn't push the issue. Joelle would wait until she got into the family before she started working with the other ladies in the family as matchmakers.

A knock came at the door. Joelle expected her mother to come busting through the door with last-minute commentary on the good, the bad, and the ugly of what was taking place out there. Although with her mother, she knew that nothing could be wrong. Her mother would have it no other way. If something went wrong, Mrs. Jamison would have heads rolling. Even with the short notice, she was determined to make this the wedding of the century. Joelle was getting her hair done when there was a knock at her door. Justine opened it and Joelle locked eyes with her brother Jacob.

Tears started to well up in her eyes as he stepped into the room wearing one of the same tuxedos as her other two brothers. It was tentative as to whether he would show or not. Jonah stated that when he last spoke with Jacob, Jacob was on the right track with getting his life back in order. Joelle was hoping he would come, but she understood his reservations. Before she could say a word, Jacob crossed the room and embraced her. Even though she had just got her makeup done, she did not care. Seeing him was the best wedding present she could receive. Jacob explained that he would not have missed her big day for the world, but he did explain that he would be leaving immediately after the reception.

Joelle was tempted to ask him to stay, but she decided that it was enough that he was here now. She knew he would open up and share when he was ready—like Xeria did with Xaviar. When Xaviar told her Xeria's story, she couldn't believe what he was saying. She was just happy his sister was okay and everything worked out well and was in her favor. She kissed Jacob on the cheek and watched as he turned and walked out. She watched him through the glass balcony doors as he made his way over to where the other two Jamison brothers were standing under the floral arch. She knew without a doubt that Jacob would be okay. She knew that God was in control and watching out for all of them. After her makeup artist reapplied her makeup, she took a glimpse of herself in the mirror. She hoped X would be pleased.

X couldn't tie his tie correctly. He was getting frustrated with every attempt. Xavian could sense that his brother needed assistance. Even though X was well over thirty, Xavian felt a sense of satisfaction knowing that no matter how old X was, he would still need his older brother. X relinquished control of the dang thing and graciously allowed his brother to assist with his tie. Xavian shared some of his anxieties on his wedding day. As X listened, he reminisced back to that day. Xavian was a mess. He couldn't get anything right. He couldn't tie his bowtie or his shoe. At one point, Xavian started crying and declaring his undying love for his future wife.

X threatened to punch him in the gut if he didn't pull himself together. Xavian kept it together until the vows. He cried so much, their father had to give him his handkerchief and Xavier's after Xavian soaked all three with tears and snot balls. At some point today, X got so emotional he thought he was about to break out in tears as well. He started to feel what Xavian was feeling. After Xavian fixed his tie, X decided to get some air. He took a walk. He couldn't believe in less than twenty minutes, he would officially be a married man. The thought of spending the rest of his life with Joelle was something he was looking forward to. X sent up a prayer thanking God for all the blessings he showered him with over this past year.

First a bookstore, then Joelle, and last a healed sister. X somehow found himself wandering over to the other side of the hotel where the bridal suite and wedding was going to take place. At first he thought that the idea of having their wedding at an outside venue in a hotel instead of at his father's church was a little too much, but now he was glad he conceded. His father would officiate the ceremony and God is everywhere. X kissed his hand and placed it on the door that his bride-to-be was behind. At that moment, he knew that today was going to be wonderful. It truly was the first day of what promised to be a blessed life with the woman that God had created especially for him. His happily ever after was about to start in less than ten minutes.

Epilogue

Xeria could barely keep her eyes open during her Gambling Anonymous meeting. She did manage to get in four hours of sleep after witnessing the most extravagant wedding between her brother and his new bride, Joelle. The affair would be the talk of the town for months to come, or until the next well-to-do African American family tried to "keep up with the Jones," or in this case "the Jamisons." However, while all eyes were on the happy couple, Xeria had her eyes on one of the groomsmen.

He had the cutest dimple on his left cheek. Every time he smiled, Xeria had visions of kissing not only that dimple, but those full lips that screamed handle with care. She had met Jonah during the wedding rehearsal the night before the wedding. As usual, Xeria was late. Her father texted her twice to get her ETA. For an older gentleman and a preacher, Xeria was still amazed at just how much her father was up on the newest technology. He even went so far as to put his beloved church on Facebook and made sure its status was updated at least once a week. He had a weekly post titled Pastor's Wisdom Corner where he would share important messages about happiness. Xeria, like her siblings, thought her father should write a book, but he would brush them off.

When Xeria walked into the rehearsal, all heads turned towards her direction. Instead of being embarrassed, she confidently walked over to where the bridesmaids were and stood in the back of the line. They were all at the altar waiting to exit. Being the tallest of the three, she knew that it was where her future sister-in-law would place her in the wedding line-up. The moment X brought Joelle to the family dinner for introductions and to announce their engagement, Xeria could tell that she was truly her brother's Eve, his rib. She liked her immediately and knew she would be a good fit with Xeria and her other sister-in-law.

She peeked around the other two bridesmaids to try to catch Joellle's eye to let her know she was sorry for her tardiness. Joelle looked back and smiled at her and all of Xeria's anxiety was immediately released. She looked down to straighten out her dress. When she looked up, she saw the wedding coordinator signal that it was her turn to exit down the aisle with her designated groomsman. She had been so preoccupied with getting there on time and making things right with

Joelle, she hadn't had a chance to check out the rest of the bridal party. She moved up in the line and looked up into the face of someone who could be described with one word: yummy. This man standing right in front of her was all sorts of fine. He was tall and resembled Joelle.

Xeria remembered X saying that both he and Joelle wanted as many siblings in the wedding party as possible. Joelle asked Xeria to be a bridesmaid and X asked two of Joelle's brothers to be the groomsmen. While caught up in her own thoughts, she failed to see that he was checking her out almost as much as she was checking him out. She smiled and slipped her arm under his awaiting arm and was led out to the church foyer with the rest of the bridal party. Once there, he was reluctant to let her arm go. When he did, he turned to her and introduced himself.

"Hi, I'm Jonah. You must be Xaviar's sister, Xeria," he stated.

Jonah was told that Xeria was beautiful, but that term did not do her enough justice. This woman was exquisite. Joelle and Xeria had an engagement party where the bridal party could meet one another. Jonah joked with his sister about not pairing him up with the "ugly betty," even if it was only for a walk up and down the aisle, a few pictures, and a bridal party dance. She promised him that all of her bridesmaids were more than pleasing to the eye; he would be more than pleased with the partner she selected for him.

"How do you know my name?" Xeria asked even though she already knew the answer.

She was almost certain that she was talked about as the only missing member of the bridal party at the engagement party. Xeria wanted to be there, but she was still recuperating from the final confrontation with Deval. It left her with ribs that were so badly broken that it required that she be hospitalized for a month, another month of bed rest, two brothers with police records, and a badly damaged cabin in the Poconos. She was grateful she had a family that would go to hell and back to keep her safe. Before Jonah could respond, one of the other groomsmen called him over. Xeria could tell it was another one of Joelle's brothers. Before excusing himself, he made Xeria promise she would not move before he got back. Xeria had never felt such a strong attraction to any man before. It was like they were magnets that were kept apart far too long. She watched as he strolled with all the confidence, daring her not to watch his swagger as he left. She was so caught up in his exit that she didn't notice that her father walked up from behind her.

"I see something or should I say someone has caught your eye," James stated.

When Xeria opened her mouth to respond to his comment, she felt a sharp pain. It had been three months since the incident. She thought she had completely healed, but apparently she hadn't. James noticing her daughter's pain calmly escorted her out of the church. He transported her to the hospital to get checked out. She wasn't discharged until 4:00 a.m. the morning of the wedding. Even with the bed rest, she managed to reopen one of her many sutures that have been in for the duration of the three months. Xeria was praising God for the rebirth of Deval since getting saved the night of the incident, but he really did a job on her the night he found her in the cabin. He was so angry. He felt his actions were justified because he loved her. If this was love, Xeria didn't want any part of it.

James called from the hospital to assure her two brothers and Joelle that Xeria was okay and that they should not cancel the wedding. Her ribs were re-wrapped and she was given pain killers that would keep her comfortable the duration of the wedding. Not one to use any type of drugs, she only agreed to take them because it would be a long day since it was an evening wedding. She was instructed to stay in bed until 4:00 p.m. When she woke up, she carefully got dressed, took the pain relievers, and was taken to the hotel by her sister-in-law, Julia. When she arrived at the venue, she had just enough time to get her hair and makeup done. She was able to make it through the ceremony. Jonah, unaware of why she left the rehearsal dinner, was aware enough to see that she was in some sort of pain.

He was very careful with her during the festivities throughout the day including walking her down the bridal path twice to and from the altar, the introduction of the bridal party at the reception, and a thirty-second bridal party two-step to their designated chairs at the head table. Xeria remained in her designated seat throughout most of the evening. As much as she wanted to dance with Jonah again and with the rest of the bridal party, she was encouraged by all, including Jonah that is might be best for her to rest. As the night progressed, Xeria enjoyed watching X retrieve the garter from the blushing bride's thigh and then toss it to the waiting gentlemen. She thought one of the Jamison brother's would catch it; instead it was a striking gentleman that was one of Xaviar's college buddies. Jonah had just missed it and seemed disappointed. He turned his piercing hazel eyes on Xeria. Instead of looking away, she kept his gaze as if they were playing a game of chicken to see who would look away first. He did.

The bride and groom said their goodbyes and left for their honeymoon around 12:00 a.m. Xeria not wanting to leave was again advised by her family that she needed to get home and get some rest. She said her goodbyes with the last one going to Jonah. Her brother Xavian dropped her off and made sure she was tucked in before going home to his wife and twins. Even though she was in bed by 1:00 a.m., she could not fall asleep. It was partly because of a slight pain, and partly due to thoughts of unfinished business with Jonah. She finally drifted off to sleep at 4:00 a.m. Before she knew it, it was 8:00 a.m. and time for her to get up for work. As much as she wanted to call out, she knew that if she did, she would be put back on probation. She couldn't afford that since she really needed this job. Even though she had long stopped gambling, she still owed people money, namely her father.

When he found out about her gambling problem and that his deacon loaned her money and became her sponsor, he was happy the rumors about her and the deacon were not true. James was not happy about having to pay off Xeria's debts, but he was glad his daughter was not an adulteress. Xeria managed to make it through the work day. She turned the key to her apartment and entered at 5:00 p.m. As much as she wanted to take a nap, she knew if she lay down, she would not get up to attend her GA meeting. She grabbed a sandwich and was back out the door. During the break after the last speaker's testimony, Xeria got up and walked to the back of the room to get a cup of much-needed coffee. The whole time she sat there, thoughts of Jonah filled her mind. She dismissed those thoughts. She couldn't fathom ever seeing him again until Joelle and X decided to have a child. Holidays or baby showers would be the only time where both extended families would meet up.

The facilitator called them back to the meeting area for the last testimony of the night. When he motioned to the man in the fourth row to come to the podium, Xeria was kind of excited to hear his story. Since she started coming to the meetings, she watched this man from behind only. She desperately wanted to lay eyes on him. Thus far she has not gotten the chance because she often got there late. Then she skipped out of the meeting ten minutes prior to its ending. She took a few more sips, tossed her cup, and took her seat. He stood up and slowly faced the audience. Before he could introduce himself aloud, he caught sight of her and gasped. He went on to tell his story. Halfway through, he started sobbing. At that moment, Xeria wanted to rush to his side and discard the falling tears that freely slid down his cheeks. The applause erupted soon after he spoke his last word. Xeria removed a tissue from her purse as he made his way over to her. He passed several fellow gamblers and received a much-needed pat on the back or man hug. When he reached her, she took the tissue and delicately wiped his face.

"What are you doing here, Jonah?"